DARK PHOENIX

PHOENIX #2

ELISE FABER

SNARKY BOOKS FOR SNARKY MINDS

DARK PHOENIX
BY ELISE FABER
Newsletter sign-up

This is a work of fiction. Names, places, characters, and events are fictitious in every regard. Any similarities to actual events and persons, living or dead, are purely coincidental. Any trademarks, service marks, product names, or named features are assumed to be the property of their respective owners, and are used only for reference. There is no implied endorsement if any of these terms are used. Except for review purposes, the reproduction of this book in whole or part, electronically or mechanically, constitutes a copyright violation.

PHOENIX SERIES

Phoenix Rising

Dark Phoenix

Phoenix Freed

ONE

"UP!"

Daughtry blinked sleep from her eyes, hazily registering Cody's concerned face.

"Up. *Now*," he ordered, throwing back the blankets.

"What—?" The flashing lights and pealing sirens finally penetrated her sleep-fogged mind.

She was out of bed before Cody had a chance to respond.

"Easy, cowgirl."

She steadied as he spoke to her across their mental link, the warm feelings of love and strength pouring down the bond to comfort her.

"A drill?" she asked, hopeful.

There'd been many drills in the two months since the Dalshie—monsters who used dark magic—had stormed the Colony and kidnapped her. So many, she thought, that her fellow Rengalla might have become complacent.

For her, complacence wouldn't ever an issue.

She'd almost been raped the first time she'd heard the alarms, cornered by the Dalshie while Cody fought to get to her.

That all-encompassing fear, the bone-deep panic, wasn't all that easy to shed.

Cody handed her a sweatshirt and cupped her cheek for a split second after she'd pulled it over her head. "If it's a drill, it's not on my schedule."

She slipped her feet into shoes, grabbed her phone, and followed him to the door.

"I can get to the basement on my own."

As a LexTal, Cody's first responsibility was the protection of their people, the Rengalla, and their home, the Colony. She could walk down two flights of stairs herself.

"I'm not going to remind you what happened the last time you tried to walk down stairs by yourself," Cody said. He pulled her into his side and kept her close.

The corridors were crowded as everyone proceeded along their assigned paths.

With its steel-reinforced walls and escape route, the basement was the safest place for them to be when the Colony was under attack.

Attack.

The word changed the direction of Cody's thoughts, and she frowned.

"I hear that, you know," she muttered.

"I know," he said and though his mind shifted to other things, he was unapologetic. "You know that the only hope we have to defeat the Dalshie is through Bond Magic."

"We're not going there." She held the door to the basement open for a young mother and her son.

"We need to go there some time," Cody murmured then turned to the boy. "Hey Danny," he said. "You got your guys?"

"Yup." Danny held up his superhero backpack, full to the brim with action figures and comic books. "I'm prepared this time."

Daughtry felt a sting at that. It was her fault that the Rengalla were going through this, up at all hours, constantly pushed from their rooms so that she could be safe.

Maybe it would be better if she lived away from the Colony. Like her mother had. Like the other Oracles before her.

"*Stop.*" Cody squeezed her waist.

"*It's the truth,*" she thought. "*This mess is because of me. If the Dalshie didn't care about my powers they—*"

"*They'd have come after us for something else. They never needed a reason before you.*" A pause. "*And you're not the only reason they're coming now.*"

She sighed but didn't argue. Because one—there wasn't really a point; her man was stubborn as hell, and two—a small part of her believed him.

Not everything was always about her.

"Just most of it, cowgirl." He flashed her a grin at her pert look, pressed a kiss to the top of her head, then shoved her into the room. "Now sit tight. I'll be back soon."

With a nod, she let him close the door, trying not to listen to his footsteps as he walked away. The scuffing of his boots depressed her, made her feel more than a little useless. Like a freaking doll on a shelf.

Her lack of training and knowledge about military strategy or even just clearing a building made her a liability. She might be the strongest Rengallan at the Colony because of her ability to access all three levels of magic—Elemental or Primary, Secondary, and Tertiary—but her refusal and her *fear* to use her magic was why she was locked in the basement with the four-year-olds.

Torching rooms, almost killing her friends, her bondmate, all made a girl nervous. She couldn't risk tapping into her powers because every time she'd attempted to use them, they'd spiraled out of control.

Sighing, she crossed over to where Suz sat on a plush leather sofa and sank down next to her friend.

Even more than her magic overwhelming her was the darkness that came along with her powers. Every time she used them a dark voice welled up inside her, encouraging her to manipulate things she had no right to mess with. It called to a hidden part of her mind. One that reveled in destruction, in causing pain and suffering.

Down that road led a rapid descent into madness.

It had driven every past Oracle into darkness, caused tainted magic to course through their veins, infecting them and turning them into Dalshie.

"Hey," Suz said, bumping her shoulder against Daughtry's. "Where did you go?"

"What? Nowhere." Then because the Colony's main healer was a dog to a bone when it came down to get information she wanted, Daughtry used the best tool in her arsenal—distraction. "How was your date?"

Suz narrowed her eyes. "You did *not* just say that." Her brown hair swung around her head as her gaze whipped around the room. "If he heard you . . . I swear to God, Dee." She made a slicing motion across her throat.

Daughtry chuckled, some of her moroseness fading. Her life wasn't perfect, far from it actually, but things were so much better than just a couple months before.

This—bantering with a friend, finding a place where she felt normal—had been a huge part of that.

"What about me?" Cody asked across the bond.

She smiled, a real one this time. Suz took one look at her face and groaned. "He can't leave you alone for five minutes?"

She laughed, holding up a hand to stop Suz's next statement. Sometimes having Cody talk into her mind and having a conversation out loud at the same time was too much.

Too much noise. Too much sensory input.

She paused for a second as she tried to remember Cody's question.

"Of course you're important," she replied. *"There. I've stroked your ego. Feel important now?"*

He laughed. *"Yes."*

"Good. Now go, concentrate," she thought. *"I don't know how you can multitask so well. I'm supposed to have that ability. I have the two X chromosomes."*

"It's all instinct, sweetheart." His mental tone told her she'd get a taste of that instinct later.

Her teeth nibbled on her lip as the memory of what he'd done with her just hours before flowed through her mind.

Cody groaned. *"Don't do that,"* he thought. *"I always feel that little sting of pain and want to soothe it with my tongue, my—"*

"I'll see you soon," she thought before he could take that description any further.

He was working and she was in a room full of people.

Nothing lay down that mental path aside from embarrassment and disappointment.

He chuckled along the bond before focusing his full attention back onto his surroundings. The LexTals had finished the interior sweep and would soon be proceeding to the exterior. Then everyone could get back to bed.

"Your date?" she asked aloud, glancing up at her friend.

"It wasn't a date and you know it. But"—Suz smiled—"whatever you call it, I had the *best* time."

She put her hand up for a high five and the loud *crack* of the doctor's palm against her own made her lips curve. "When do you go out again?"

"Tomorrow."

If she wasn't mistaken, Suz's cheeks had become a little flushed.

"We're going to take a walk through the gardens then watch a movie in one of the common rooms." The doctor shrugged. "It's totally juvenile, but I'm excited."

"I'm happy for you—" she started but her words cut off on a gasp when a bolt of emotion shot through the bond.

"What is it?" Suz asked, dropping to her knees in front of Daughtry.

"It's—"

There was too much pain.

Her eyes filled with tears, her brain with images as she connected with Cody's mind—

He was outside. The grass was wet, seeping through his jeans. His hands trembled.

"*Cody?*" she asked.

He didn't respond. Was he hurt? She delved deeper into his mind.

No, not hurt just—*shocked?*

Her eyes saw what he saw, and his emotions tangled with her own. Fear. Anger. Hope. Disappointment.

A burst of noise had him looking up, drawing his weapon.

John and Morgan flanked him, magic crackling from their palms.

A woman stepped out of the trees, her delicate features and cherry-red hair an identical match to the prone female on the ground.

Closer, the woman from the trees stepped, her lips curled up into a cruel smile that was all too familiar. This was the woman who'd kidnapped Daughtry, who'd tortured her.

She morphed in front of Cody, hair darkening, turning more mahogany than cherry, her eyes no longer green but—

"*Consider my message delivered,*" she said, laughing as a nest of black strands of magic burst from her palms and surrounded her. A heartbeat later, she was gone. Cody stared at the red-haired woman on the ground, afraid to hope.

"*Caroline,*" he gasped then hugged her close.

TWO

"OH GOD!" Daughtry gasped, shooting to her feet. Suz followed. "We need supplies. We need a bed. We need—"

"Hey." Suz grabbed her arms. "Slow down. What happened? Who's hurt?"

"Caroline." Daughtry shook her off and ran for the door. The infirmary was only one floor up and she could open it herself. Surely Caroline would need it with the amount of bruises and cuts covering her body.

"Caroline?" The utter incredulity in the doctor's tone was what finally slowed Daughtry down.

Because Suz hadn't seen the other woman—the other Caroline. Hadn't seen the woman who'd stood above Cody's sister or the way her disguise had melted away, how green eyes had darkened and cherry-red hair turned mahogany.

Daughtry's throat burned and it took everything in her to not puke up her dinner right there in front of everyone. The woman who'd teleported away in a net of black magic had looked like—

Her.

Delicate bone structure, similar hair color, and the eyes . . .

A twin? A cousin? A sister? Did Daughtry have a relative that no one knew about?

She shook herself. *That* didn't matter right now. What did was that an innocent woman—oh, please let her be innocent—was injured and needed help. Caroline was the only person in his family to truly accept Cody . . . at least until she had moved up in the ranks and taken the position of Councilhead—

Though, seeing as how Cody's sister had just been dumped off at the Colony like a heap of trash, who knew how much of that had been Daughtry's potential relative and how much had been Caroline herself.

Panic gripped her for a moment before she regained control. She needed to be calm, to not add to Cody's tangled emotions. They could all take time to understand the implications of what Caroline's reappearance meant later. What was important in that moment, if Caroline *was* indeed innocent, was for the only person in Cody's family who'd ever accepted him to get well.

She was going to make that happen.

"Come on." With a quick movement, she grabbed Suz's arm and tugged her out into the hallway, away from the curious eyes and gossiping tongues. News would get out soon enough but Daughtry didn't exactly revel in being that evening's entertainment.

Suz waited until they were heading upstairs before she asked, "What the hell is going on, Dee?"

"It wasn't Caroline." Daughtry gave the bond a quick mental check. Cody had stayed with Caroline as the rest of the LexTals checked the surrounding area for more Dalshie. Releasing their link, she turned her focus to Suz. "Caroline is outside. The real one. The other Caroline, the one who turned, I don't think that was actually *our* Caroline."

Which was the most convoluted explanation ever, but Suz seemed to understand. "A glamour?"

That was probably the best explanation, but the sheer amount of power it would have taken for the woman to keep it constantly in place—the disguise running so deep as to even change the color of her magic—*that* was frightening. "That's the only thing I can think of."

Suz appeared to be grappling with the facts laid out in front of them. "Dalshie can make themselves look human, use their powers to hide the signs of infection," she said. "But I've never heard of a Dalshie being able to actually change the appearance of their magic or alter themselves so much that they resembled a completely different person."

Daughtry hadn't either, but she was new to this whole magical being thing. "There's nothing about in the books I've studied. We know how to destroy Dalshie, but taking the time to talk with them and understand the inner workings of their minds—"

A wry smile crossed Suz's lips. "Kind of hard to study something that's trying to kill you."

"Seriously." She'd had her fair share of Dalshie interactions and every one of the red-eyed, black-palmed monsters had been cruel, had reveled in the pain and suffering of others. They weren't exactly up for small talk.

They were strong, yes, could heal in the blink of an eye, and the only way to kill them was with a knife to the heart or decapitation.

So chit-chat wasn't on the menu.

"Then . . . it wasn't Caroline who kidnapped you?" Suz asked.

"Yes." She bit her lip. Maybe. Hopefully. Okay, dammit, it *had* to be. Cody needed to have *one* break in his life. His entire family couldn't all be jerks.

"Okay then." Suz shifted into doctor mode. "She was hurt? Where? How badly?"

As Daughtry relayed what she'd seen through Cody's mind, the doctor's face grew more and more serious. For good reason. The massive amount of injuries was life threatening.

But that Caroline was injured was a good sign.

It was what gave Daughtry hope that her first instinct about Caroline being innocent was true. Cody's sister might not have turned into their enemy because she *was* hurt.

A Dalshie had powers the Rengalla didn't. They could heal any injuries—the smallest scratch to the most grievous—in an instant.

"Let's get set up," Suz said as she slapped her hand on the lock panel for the infirmary. Wisps of chocolate brown magic slipped from her skin and crawled onto the metal. A moment later, they heard a soft *click* of the lock disengaging before Suz let the magic slip away.

Daughtry followed her down the hall and into the trauma room where they began laying out supplies. Gauze, saline, tweezers. Anything Suz might need in the healing process.

Because if Caroline was as bad off as she appeared through Cody's mind then Suz might not have enough power to heal her all at once.

"Internal injuries will be a concern," the doctor murmured to herself. "Surface cuts and abrasions will have to be taken care of too, but after." She glanced up. "Where are they?"

Daughtry had been keeping half an eye on Cody through the bond. They'd finished the sweep and were heading inside.

"Cody?" He didn't respond but she felt his attention slowly focus onto her. *"Bring her to the infirmary. Suz is ready for her."*

"Got it," he said before his consciousness slipped back across their link.

"They'll be here in just a couple of minutes."

Suz nodded and checked over the supplies, her almost detached doctor's persona in full effect. It was a good response, the mental state that helped her categorize and remember a million things all at the same time.

After opening a cabinet, Suz pulled out another bin. "Can you grab more gauze from Exam Room Two? I don't think this is enough."

"Sure." Daughtry headed down the hall.

"Oh, and a few more suture kits."

"Got it."

She grabbed what Suz had asked for and started to head back, her hands full, when the door burst open.

Cody was in the lead, his sister in his arms. Tyler, another LexTal and her friend, stood behind him, exhaustion written into the deep lines around his mouth and eyes, his gait the slightly unsteady one of someone who'd use a lot of magic recently. She knew he had been on several missions as of late and that the work was emotionally and physically taxing.

After reassuring herself that he was okay, she forced her eyes back to Cody's then down to the woman she'd avoided looking at.

Somehow Caroline appeared worse in person than she had through the distillation of Cody's mind. Daughtry throat tightened, eyes filling with tears.

Caroline had been mutilated, her body utterly decimated. Not one inch of her exposed skin—and there was a lot of it, the rags that were trying to pass as clothes hardly covering anything —was free of blood or cuts or bruises.

Cody's stare met hers, freezing her in place when she would have hurried toward him. Her tongue stuck to the roof of her mouth and her legs wobbled.

Because he looked furious.

But that wasn't what made unease settle into every crevice of her body. He wasn't just angry.

No. Cody was furious . . . at *her*.

His mind slammed into hers—pissed off, intense, filled with a rage that cooled her blood to ice. His eyes, emerald and usually so warm when they met hers, had regressed back into the frigid depths that had pierced straight through her soul when they'd first met.

She stared at him, unable to speak as dread swelled up.

He raised a brow and waited for another second before snapping, "Dammit, Daughtry. Which room?"

"Oh–uh." She fumbled with the supplies as his sharp tone scoured her skin. "Room—"

"Right here," Suz said as she emerged from the trauma room. Cody followed her back inside without another glance back. A roll of gauze slipped out of her hands, started to fall. She made a grab for it and ended up dropping everything else in the process.

"Shit," she murmured, crouching down to pick everything up.

"You okay?"

John's voice made her jump.

"Oh," she said, forcing lightness into her voice. "I didn't see you come in."

"Dee." He'd been her friend before she knew about her magic, and they had a connection that ran deeper than surface level.

Hence, he knew she was bullshitting.

She straightened her shoulders, forced herself to calm. Her mind was raw from Cody's emotions, the drama of the situation. That was all. "I'm always okay."

But she couldn't deny her stomach was tight with nerves. These last few months with Cody had been wonderful and she was desperately trying to swallow down the feeling that everything might have changed over the course of half an hour.

"It's got to be tough." Her head whipped up, took in John's

kind, intuitive expression. The damn man needed to stop doing that. "Seeing her. After what was done to you."

Images of the kidnapping flooded through her mind—the fear, the blood, the darkness snaking through her. She shook her head to ward them off. "I'm fine."

John opened his mouth to say something but Suz beat him to it.

"Need those supplies, Dee," the doctor called through the open door.

"Coming!" Daughtry called back, grateful to avoid John's penetrating gaze.

She stepped across the threshold and into chaos. Cody and Dee stood next to Caroline's bed. Supplies were torn open, used and stained gauze littered all over the floor. Emerald strands of magic had emerged from Cody's palms, wrapping their way over Caroline's prone form and knitting together wounds by the half dozen.

Suz's brown strands were focused on Caroline's skull, the colored threads sitting atop Caroline's hair before disappearing as they delved into the injuries below the skin.

"Her brain is swelling," Suz said to no one in particular. "Dammit, Cody. You need to work faster. I can't . . ." She trailed off as she poured more magic into Caroline.

Daughtry set her supplies on the table then turned to Cody.

"Take it," she said.

He didn't pause to look at her, to say anything. He just reached into her mind and took every bit of magic she had at her disposal.

Her legs went weak at the sudden departure and she gave a little cry as her knees hit the ground hard. Someone put a hand under her arm and guided her to a chair—well, more like carried her, since her mind was spinning and she felt too weak to walk.

"Cody?" she asked on a whisper.

"Let me get you some ice." The words were just as soft, but not from the man she wanted to talk to. Of course Cody wouldn't leave his sister, not Caroline's situation was too fragile. What he was doing was too important.

She slit open her eyes, waiting as the room tilted then steadied before trying to assure John. "I'm okay." *Or close enough.*

"Your knees." Gentle fingers straightened her legs.

She looked down and grimaced. Black bruises were already emerging on her bare knees and one was cut, blood dripping down her shin.

Next time she took a spill, she'd plan on wearing pants not flimsy pajama shorts.

"They're fine," she said. "I should have been ready."

John grunted. "He should have warned you."

Maybe. But she wasn't going to admit it. "I told him to take it," she said, and if it was a touch defensive, now wasn't the time to acknowledge it. "My knees are fine."

Except they were already starting to throb. So was her head, as it struggled to deal with the sudden loss of magic. Her power was regenerating, but slowly, a trickle in the back of her mind. It would be a couple hours until she was whole again.

"Of course they are," John agreed then stood and grabbed a pair of ice packs anyway, setting them gently against her aching knees.

Biting back a wince and rolling her eyes mentally, Caroline was in much worse shape. Besides, she'd been kidnapped, beaten up, knocked down a flight of stairs, and it was a few bruises that felled her? A two-year-old would whine less than her.

"You're not whining, Dee," John said, glancing up to meet her eyes. "You never complain."

Odd.

She was almost certain she hadn't actually said that aloud, but maybe the stress of the evening was getting to her. The bond was stronger than ever. It shielded her from John's telepathy picking up on her thoughts and prevented any unwanted visions.

The plastic of the ice packs crinkled as she shifted them around on her knees. "Apparently you haven't heard me when the Commissary is out of Diet Coke," she said.

"Oh no, not that." His hands brushed hers away as he moved to hold the ice in place. It wasn't the heat or comfort of Cody's touch, but it was the kindness she'd always associated with him. "Sweetheart." He waited until she met his eyes. "Everything is fine."

She wanted to protest, the churning in her gut and the distance in her bond making her wary.

But she trusted John.

He'd been there for her, had once given her the news that her ex-fiancé was breaking up with her, had put his life on the line for her when the Dalshie first began pursuing her.

His determination to keep her safe was the only reason she'd even made it to the Colony.

"More gauze," Suz barked.

Daughtry set the ice packs aside, shoved herself to her feet, and hurried to fulfill the order.

Caroline and Cody needed her.

She was going to be there for them. No matter what.

THREE

BUT A FEW DAYS LATER, Daughtry was worried.

Cody stood in front of her—towered, really—his eyes icy. It was the first time he'd been in their quarters since Caroline had been brought in, the first time he'd spared Daughtry more than a brief glance.

The large, luxurious bedroom and bathroom combination that was the Rengallan equivalent a one-bedroom apartment had been empty without him.

Understandably, he'd been keeping vigil over his sister and completing his LexTal duties, while she'd been doing her best to juggle her studies and making sure Cody got enough food and sleep.

It was a futile task, as when Cody wasn't doing his part to protect the Colony, he hadn't left Caroline's bedside. But Daughtry had thought she'd been balancing everything pretty well.

This confrontation spoke to the opposite.

"Why didn't you tell me?" he demanded.

His tone made her straighten in the leather office chair, scattering a few papers and pencils to the plush carpeting. She bent down, retrieved them, then placed the notes back atop the large solid wood desk. It was a moment before she could will herself turn to face Cody.

Frustration and anger poured out of him, rubbing her skin raw. His mind was a hot poker against hers, the bond pulsing as his emotions drove into her.

It was intense. It was unwelcome.

Intellectually, she understood Cody was scared that Caroline hadn't woken up yet, furious that the Dalshie had harmed her so terribly.

But she didn't like that he was taking his worry out on her.

She had nothing to do with it.

Except that the woman who'd left Caroline just outside the Colony's shield might be related to her—their shared physical resemblance something all the LexTals had noticed, though few had actually commented on it.

The freaking elephant in the room.

If Daughtry had a relative, she didn't know what form that relation might come in. Her mother was dead. She had no siblings or cousins to speak of. Was the resemblance coincidence? Another Dalshie manipulation? Because if the Dalshie could make themselves look like Caroline, they could replicate Daughtry's appearance.

However, if it *wasn't* a cruel trick—

Her stomached knotted and she sucked in a breath of air. Even if the Dalshie *was* related to her, it didn't matter. Black magic eliminated every trace of the person they'd been before.

Not to mention, she didn't shoulder any responsibility for their actions, no matter the potential of shared DNA.

"Why didn't you tell me?" Cody asked again.

"Tell you *what* exactly?" Her voice was calm in spite of her fragile emotions and Cody's intense ones.

His eyes flashed away, then back. "Why didn't you tell me

that Caroline was there. A prisoner." His coughed as he got a little choked up. "Tortured."

"I didn't know." It was a whisper. She extended a hand, wanting to touch him, to comfort him.

His fist descended and slammed against the desktop. The loud *crack* made her start. "How?" he asked. "How did you *not* know?"

"Cody." Bracing herself—this *was* Cody after all, she had nothing to fear from him—she laid a hand on his chest. Her heart was racing and the sight of that fist descending still played in her mind.

No, he would *never* hurt her.

But for a second, the fury in his mind, on his face had made her nervous.

"*Of course* I didn't know. You can see my soul, could know my every thought if you wanted. But more than that, you *know* me better than anyone else." Her voice dropped to a whisper. "Do you honestly think I would keep something like that from you?"

He didn't respond.

They stood there, the silence worse for her nerves than the smothering blackness of a small, dark hole. All the little doubts that had been held at bay when she and Cody committed to each other began to creep back in.

If he didn't trust she would have said something—

"I believe you," he said, gently grasping her hand, lifting it to rest behind his neck. The touch, the first in seven days, almost made her weak with relief. He wrapped his arms around her waist and tugged her against his chest.

Then he just held her for a long moment.

Finally, she got the sense that after a week of distance—a week of Cody alternating between patrols and spending every free moment next to his sister's bed, a week where she'd hardly seen him for longer than five minutes, a week where he'd barely spoken to her—that things would be okay.

"Let's go to bed," he said, his work-roughened hands teasing as he stripped her out of her clothes, though she could tell from the bond sex wasn't his intent. A second later he handed her one of his T-shirts, her favored sleepwear, and fresh panties from a drawer.

After she was dressed, he tucked her under the covers and cupped her cheek, rubbing his thumb over the skin there. "I love you."

Her eyes slid closed from the pleasure of the words, the caress. But then it was gone. They flashed back open at the sound of the door to the hallway closing.

"Where are you going?" she thought.

"The infirmary."

"Oh. Well, if you need anything—"

"I won't."

"Okay." She paused. *"I love you, too."* The words drifted along the bond, hanging suspended and unheard because Cody's mind had focused elsewhere.

It took a long time to fall asleep. And when she did, it was with wet cheeks.

"You NEED TO EAT," she said a couple of days later, through the closed bathroom door.

Cody's sister still hadn't woken and Daughtry was worried by the sheer amount of weight he'd lost, by the fatigue she could sense through the bond.

"Cody?" she asked through the bond.

It seemed to take a long time for her hail to reach him and even longer for him to respond. *"Yeah?"*

"I have your favorite cereal out here," she said with a smile. He'd once brought her an impromptu picnic of cereal and milk and the memory was one that she held close. She'd hoped he'd remember, that it might coax him out of some of his worry, that—

"Stop thinking so hard," his mental voice snapped. *"You're giving me a headache."*

She froze, hands shaking as she clutched the bowl. *"Sorry, I just—"*

"Leave it on the table," he said, focus already shifting. *"I need to get back to Caroline."*

Ugliness reared up in Daughtry before she shoved it fiercely down. His sister was deathly ill and there was absolutely nothing to feel jealous about. As for the dismissive tone? Well, clearly, he had a lot on his plate with his LexTal responsibilities and everything else.

Or—

Nope. That was it, just stress from a stressful situation and—

"Cowgirl. Headache."

"Oh. Sorry."

"You should go."

She swallowed hard, nodded though he couldn't see her, and set the cereal on the desk. With a deep breath, she slipped from the room and into the hall—

"Oof."

Male hands steadied her before she could tumble to the carpet.

"Sorry," she muttered stepping back.

"It's fine," he said, and it took her a moment to discern who she'd nearly plowed down. Partly because she rarely saw the other man and partly because he was one portion of a set of three. "Morgan," he added with a smirk, just as she'd mentally identified him. He tended to wear his hair a bit longer than his brothers and his eyes had more gold.

"I know," she replied then admitted with a wry smile. "Just took me a minute."

"Happens to the best of us." He started to leave but paused mid-stride. "You okay?"

Probably because the smile she'd been holding on to had faded and no doubt some of the misery she felt about Caroline and Cody and the distance in her relationship had crept into her expression.

She would never be good at poker. Too easy to read.

And that sparked a memory, of another time, months before when Cody had used the words to hurt her, to push her away.

This was becoming an unpleasant pattern.

"I'm fine," she said, realizing that concern had crept into Morgan's expression.

"Do you—?"

"Actually," she added. "I'm late meeting someone and so I . . ."

"Need to go," he supplied when she trailed off.

"Yeah. That."

"Okay." He held her gaze for another heartbeat before turning away. "My room's just down the hall if you to talk—"

"Thanks!" she chirped. "I'll see around."

And then she hurried away, eyes burning, knowing that if Cody had showed her half the concern that Morgan, almost a stranger had, then everything would have seemed fine.

As it was, the distance along the bond made Morgan's kindness sting all that much more.

———

THE INFIRMARY WAS quiet when Daughtry entered it two days

later. Most of the Rengalla weren't early risers. Case in point, as she'd made her way to the clinic, she hadn't seen another person.

A loud *screech* behind her signaled the door closing. She winced and glanced around, hoping she hadn't disturbed Cody and Caroline. Or whoever else might be a patient.

After a moment without anyone coming out to yell at her, she relaxed. Moving past the empty reception desk where Gabby, Suz's assistant, usually sat, she made her way down the hallway.

A quick glance into exam room one told her it was unoccupied and so she began with her usual inventory of equipment and supplies.

Since the Dalshie attack, Suz had wanted to keep extra provisions on hand. Which made total sense to Daughtry. There weren't many healers: Suz, Cody, Tyler, and a few others who were less powerful. Once their magic was tapped out, it could be hours until it regenerated. Hence, they brought in enough supplies to rival any state-of-the-art hospital.

Power could be shared between Rengalla, but it wasn't very effective. She and Cody were the exception. The bond made the exchange easier, but the two of them didn't have enough juice to heal the entire Colony.

Typically, the person who was supplying the magic was tapped out almost before the person receiving the power benefited. Or they didn't let go in time and passed out from giving too much.

Still, in a pinch—an emergency—transfers worked.

However, for smaller injuries—for bruises, cuts, sometimes even broken bones—Suz put her M.D. training to use and treated her patients the old-fashioned way. Sighing, she switched to the next cabinet, wishing she could help the same way. Her basic first aid training was excellent, thanks to Suz's training, but if she had powers that healed instead of killed—

Nope, not going down there again.

With a shake of her head, she opened the cupboard, making a mental note of the items that were low. Her approach was systematic, thorough, and so it took her awhile to work her way down to exam room four.

She'd actually entered the suite and begun cataloguing the supplies before the hair rose on the back of her neck.

What she saw there simultaneously swelled her heart and riddled her with jealousy. Cody lay on the gurney, Caroline gathered in his arms.

In the end, relief won out.

The fact that Caroline had been moved from the trauma room meant she had to be doing better. She would hopefully regain consciousness soon.

Quietly, Daughtry closed the cabinet and turned to leave. But as she did so, her hip collided with the side table, a tray of metal instruments clattering to the floor.

"Shit," she muttered then hurried to pick up the tools and put them to the side so they could be disinfected.

Cody was still sleeping, so if she could just get out without them seeing her—

"You."

At Caroline's voice, she turned. Cody's sister had sat up on the gurney, her face pale but her expression alert. And furious.

So. Fucking. Furious.

"I'm Daughtry," she said with a glance towards Cody, who hadn't woken despite the racket. She nudged the bond with her mind, her version of an alarm clock. Now would be a good time for him to open his eyes. "Everyone has been so worried since you showed up. It was touch and go there for a while . . . but

Cody and Suz healed you and . . ." She was babbling and knew it.

A shove along the bond, her best effort best to rouse Cody. He didn't move.

Daughtry's gaze locked onto Caroline's. God, the anger directed at her was so fierce, so intense, and from eyes so like Cody's that it sliced open her heart.

"You bitch."

She was screwed.

But she was also determined not to screw this up. This was Cody's sister after all.

"I'm sorry I wake you," she said softly. "I'm Cody's—"

"I don't give a fuck who you're pretending to be this time," Caroline said. "All I want is to watch the life slip from your eyes."

A bolt of magic flew across the room.

If Daughtry hadn't been so shocked, she could have moved.

If the shot had been a little to the left it would have hurt, but she would have remained standing. Then the bond would have re-calibrated her shield and she would have been protected from another strike.

But as it turned out, Caroline's aim was true.

And never having been hit with Rengallan magic, Daughtry's shields were worthless for that first blow.

Caroline didn't need another.

The magic hit Daughtry dead center in the chest.

FOUR

"YOU NEED TO GIVE HER A BREAK."

The words penetrated the haze around Daughtry's mind and all at once, she crashed back into consciousness. Green magic had flown at her. A bolt of hardened fire designed to wound, to burn had collided with her—

Sitting up on a gasp, she glanced down. The skin around her heart was pink, a little raw looking, but otherwise unblemished.

Not finding a gapping hole in her torso calmed her considerably, and with a few deep breaths, she was able to take in her surroundings.

Being in the infirmary didn't surprise her half as much as the room she'd been put in.

Six? She'd been carted down the hall into the smallest room? Trying to push away the notion that she'd been Harry Pottered into the crappiest space was harder than she would have expected.

It took a moment before she could focus enough to be logical.

Suz was probably worried about Caroline going homicidal again and that was the reason they'd put Daughtry as far as possible from Cody's sister. It was the only reasonable explanation—no matter how that little voice inside of her mind whispered it was because they didn't like her, that she wasn't good enough—

"What the fuck was she doing in there at all?" Her eyes flew towards the closed door. It was Cody who'd spoken, his voice harsh and intense.

In response, there was a long pause filled with so much judgment that it seeped through the walls.

What she didn't know was if it was directed at her or at Cody.

Finally the other man spoke again—it was John, she realized, belatedly recognizing his deep baritone voice. "Barring the fact that she works here?" A humorless laugh. "You're fucking this up, dude. And I'm not the only one who's tired of seeing that wounded puppy dog expression on her face. You need to fix this."

A wave of cold washed over her, soaking into her limbs, her heart.

Her throat felt as though it were being constricted from the inside out, as if sobs were literally trying to burst out from her windpipe.

John, too? She was annoying the man who was basically patience personified?

Pathetic.

At that thought, Cody finally registered that she was awake.

His mind focused on hers like a laser, assessing her body, her emotions. And for the first time in a long time, she wanted to hide under his scrutiny. She didn't want him to see how badly John's words had affected her, how much his distance hurt.

Turning away both mentally and physically, she searched the room for her clothes. Her jeans and shoes were easy, but her shirt was nowhere to be found.

Which probably meant that it had been torched beyond salvaging.

Damn elemental magic. No. Damn *fire*. It burned everything.

A snort. Yes, she knew that much was obvious, but she was still just going with it.

Sighing, she opened the cabinet on the far right of the room, knowing it was filled with clothes the LexTals left. Small injuries were common as they trained, and they'd gotten tired of being ogled in the corridors—or *some* of them had—so they usually left a stack of T-shirts in each room.

Thankfully, the stash was still there and she rifled through the pile until she found one that smelled like the salty brine of ocean water combined with the spicy tang of pine. She'd already brought it to her nose and inhaled before she realized what she was doing.

Damn him. Cody's scent was like crack.

Shoving the shirt away, she pulled out the one below it. It had a picture of a T-Rex and said: *If you're happy and you know it clap your... oh.*

Incongruously, she laughed.

Even when he wasn't physically present, Tyler still had the ability to make her feel good. He'd been her rock when the Dalshie had kidnapped them both—her symbol of hope in a terrible situation. But most importantly, he'd befriended her from the moment he'd met her. Had been kind and funny. Sweet—

"Why don't you buy him a medal?" Cody's voice didn't make her jump, exactly. Some part of her consciousness had realized he was there, had recognized his scent. But she hadn't known that he'd been so focused on her thoughts.

For once, that closeness felt like an invasion of her privacy. Especially because they tried not to eavesdrop on each other's minds, at least not past discerning whether or not the other person was alive and okay.

Projecting her thoughts and emotions was one thing, communicating across their link another, but rifling through the so-called inner sanctum of each other's brains? *That* was something they tried to avoid.

She shrugged off the way the notion made her feel and continued getting dressed.

"Should you be out of bed?"

There was concern in his voice, worry that called to her, tried to convince her there wasn't a problem between them.

Except there *was*. And it was a whopper.

She glanced down to button her jeans and her chin rested against her chest as she spoke. "You blame me for Caroline."

It wasn't a question because she already knew the answer.

What she didn't understand was how the hell he could.

"Of course I don't," he said. "That's ridiculous. Why would you think that?"

She laughed, though not from amusement, and the sound actually hurt her ears, her heart. It was a moment before she could make herself look at him, at the face that was practically ingrained into her soul, at the man who she'd let in deeper than any other person.

Which made what he was doing hurt all that much more.

"Where have you gone?" A small part of her wanted to beg him to be the man she'd come to love again. The rest of her had been wounded by the people who were supposed to care about her too many times. So when he merely stared back at her, she shook her head. "Yeah. I thought that would be your answer."

Cody was much older than her, almost seventy years because of the extended life of the Rengalla. Her presence was merely a blip on the radar, a collection of months compared to a life that had almost reached a century.

It was impossible to compete with such a breadth of experience and memories. She would *never* compare.

"Daughtry—" he began. Then stopped.

An odd sensation settled over her when the only thing that stretched between them was silence. It wasn't numbness, not quite. Nor entirely anger.

She was just . . . done.

Done with the anguish, done with allowing herself to be hurt.

Cody had a lot of good qualities. She wasn't with him just because he was gorgeous and had a nice body. He was loyal—devoted to the LexTals and the Colony—heroic, protective, and he'd seemed to understand her in a way that no one else had ever been able.

He also didn't exactly measure his self-worth based on others.

Not like she tended to do.

A sigh passed through her lips. Damn. What a mess.

"I have to go." She started for the open door, knowing it would lead to the hallways and freedom from that cool emerald gaze, knowing it would give her a chance to get a freaking grip.

She was trying to convince herself this was simply a bump in the road that was their relationship, but what kind of person would she be if she let him treat her like this?

Weak? Pathetic? Or normal? Rational?

He caught her arm. "Hey."

She froze. The contact—in spite everything that was going wrong with them—still made every nerve on her body stand on end.

His fingers trailed over the cotton covering her collarbone and she wanted to close her eyes. This was it. This was the moment when he'd realize that *of course* she hadn't known about Caroline. That his sister's injuries weren't her fault. That—

"You all healed up?"

The words pounded through her like the final nail piercing the wood of a coffin.

Her smile was brittle, her mind retreated as far back into itself as possible. "I'm great. Thanks for the healing."

It was an assumption that he still cared about her enough to not want to watch her die in front of him.

He inclined his head. "Anytime. And Daughtry?"

"Yeah?"

"We've relocated Caroline to the suite of rooms in the basement," he said, almost formal, no sign of softness, affection. No warmth. "I'd avoid them, if I were you. At least until I've had a chance to explain about you."

"Okay."

A moment later, she was gone.

The gentle tapping of her sneakers against the hardwood floor in the deserted hallways had never sounded so lonely.

FIVE

DAUGHTRY LOOKED at the door with an inexplicable amount of nerves. She'd debated coming, was torn between avoidance and the small hope that perhaps she might one day be able to control her powers.

But with Cody—

A shake of her head cleared that line of thinking from her mind. It wasn't the time for emotions. This was her opportunity to seize her future.

To find a way to use her magic without losing her humanity, without turning into a Dalshie.

Two Rengalla turned the corner and passed behind her. She smiled and they paused, exchanged hi-how-are-you's before the other women moved on.

Daughtry didn't know their names, their powers, or anything else about them. But the friendly interchange was exactly like the hundreds of other little interactions that she had in the Colony every day. It was such a departure from the isolation of her life from a few months' prior that she couldn't help but smile.

To be accepted into a community, to be different and yet

still belong, *that* was why she felt the need to fight for her place here.

Finding a way to be useful was a piece of that.

She wanted to contribute something.

The door opened.

"Were you going to knock, my dear?" Francis asked as he regarded her. "Or remain standing there all day?" One brow lifted. It was a scholarly gesture, appropriate with his position as head teacher, and made her feel acutely incompetent.

As she scrambled for something to say, Francis smiled and gestured her inside. He directed her to a small room just off the hallway then disappeared, saying something about refreshments.

His quarters were larger than the one-bedroom variety that was hers and Cody's. They had a large bedroom, granted, with the space for a small sitting area and a desk, but they didn't have the small kitchenette where Francis was currently making tea.

A beige loveseat adorned with a colorful splash of pillows filled most of the living room. Down the hall, it looked like Francis had a bedroom and bathroom, like her, but also another area. Maybe an office, though she could only see the back of a brown leather armchair through the partially open door.

The sofa she was sitting on was covered in a soft woven fabric that felt like velvet against her bare arms. The walls were pale blue, close to the aquamarine of Francis's eyes.

Everything was orderly.

Not that she should have expected anything different, given Francis's demeanor. Steady and precise were the words she thought of when it came to him. But she'd also imagined Francis's quarters with the dark wood and leather of a masculine British manor. Plus some gold leaf and silk wallpaper to go along with his Old World features and thinning gray hair. In her head, that decor fit with his old world, tea-drinking style.

"You look dubious, dear," he said and handed her a small ceramic cup.

"Oh." She coughed. "I just wasn't expecting— " She glanced around the room, eyes stopping on a lamp that sat on a doily. A real-life, honest-to-God doily.

"Lace and velvet?" Francis finished for her.

"Um . . . yes?"

Francis chuckled. "My wife decorated these rooms."

"You're married?"

"I take it by the incredulous tone in your voice that you had suspected me to be asexual?" Francis's eyes twinkled. "I *am* married. Have been for nearly four hundred years."

That made her both simultaneously happy for him and sad for herself.

"Not all of that has been easy or joyous," he said. "But I don't regret one day of my time with Margaret."

"That's sweet."

Francis smiled. "I would like to think so." He set his cup down and gazed at her. "I'm assuming you *haven't* come to discuss my love life?"

Her cheeks creased. "Not today," she said and took a fortifying breath. "When I was kidnapped, I came to understand my powers better." Had actually been forced to use her magic or watch the Dalshie kill Tyler. "I found the key." She glanced up to find Francis watching her, his expression curious but his eyes serious. He knew the implications of her statement. "Except there were two keys," she continued. "When I pull the vision of someone dying, there are two conditions for me to manipulate. One makes it better. One that makes it worse."

There was a slight hesitation before Francis spoke. "And you think that is why you were only able to worsen the visions when your powers were blocked. Without full access to your powers, you could only locate one key."

"I think so." She hadn't had full access to her magic until the final block on her magic had disintegrated during the Dalshie's attempted rape. When she'd defended herself, the magical shield in her mind had burst and the reverberation of her powers had torched the entire room.

"I'm sorry, dear. I should have recognized that as a possibility. I had assumed that Caroline had removed—" A pause as he no doubt remembered that the woman who'd been in Daughtry's mind, purporting to help, hadn't been Cody's sister at all. "I'd assumed all of the blocks had been removed."

He tapped his fingers on his chin and she could practically feel him burrowing his way through centuries of memories and information. "I've never known an Oracle to have located two keys in their visions. Was there a difference between the two?"

That was where it got tricky.

"Yes," she said. "The first one was tempting and tried to coax me in. It wasn't until I took a closer look that I realized it would have made the death worse." She hadn't even felt the black magic. Not at first.

"And the other?"

"I *think* it was good. It seemed to bring the death about in a way that was less gruesome. It would have happened later, at the hands of someone else. " With a sigh, she stood and paced the small room. "But how do I trust it? I was fooled before. The darkness inside of me is smart. What if it coaxes me down that path without me even knowing it?"

Realizing she still clutched the teacup in her hands, which were shaking, she carefully set it down on the glass table.

Her immediate reaction to her discovery about the keys had been to cut her losses, to run—to stab herself in the heart in her own version of martyrdom.

Not smart, she knew.

But panic and being surrounded by mortal enemies tended to do that to a girl.

Still, away from the fear and risk of torture she had to admit that a large part of her wanted to control her powers. Even if she didn't alter any visions in the future, she would like to be able to go back and fix the ones she'd screwed up in the past.

"Have you ever read anything about water pollution?"

Her mind scrambled to keep up with the change in topic. "Um, yes?"

"So you've heard of biomagnification? Where a small amount of a toxin multiplies almost by a factor of ten as it moves its way up the food chain?"

She shook her head. What did this have to do with—?

"A minuscule amount of pollutant can enter a lake or river. That is then absorbed by plants, which are eaten by bugs, who are eaten by fish. Those fish are eaten by birds and so on, until the prey is consumed by the apex predator." Francis took a sip of his tea, still calmly perched on the sofa. "By that point the toxin is in such high concentration that there are grievous effects on that top predator."

"Okay . . ."

"I imagine the dark magic like that," he said. "A small drop of it infects your soul. It might be for something nearly impossible to detect but with each further act, the infection is magnified. Until it takes over."

Was he saying there was no hope for her? This wasn't quite the pep talk she'd been imagining.

". . . Yet, in some ecosystems there might be a bacteria that can consume the toxin without ill effect and the food chain stays intact."

She paused in her pacing, and stared at him. "You're saying that I might have bacteria?"

"What I'm saying is that not everyone is the same." He

smiled. "Our powers come from the elements, so at our root we try to follow the natural system of the world. We might have the power to manipulate storms or create thousands of pounds of gold, but we try not to muck with the natural system of things. Because the world in balance means that *we're* in balance."

He was losing her. "But we use magic all of the time. We use fire and healing and—"

"This is where we'd talk micro versus macro." He chuckled. "You use your magic to start a campfire and that has little to no effect on the world. But use that same magic to burn down a forest? The implications are much larger."

"I'm confused," she admitted.

Her magic was derived from the elements, she got that. But what else? She should just try not to screw up the planet?

"The micro is you," Francis told. "Your mini-ecosystem. In balance, you can use elemental magic. Out of balance—polluted—it becomes something else."

"Dalshie."

"Yes," he agreed. "They're still powerful because at the root they are Rengalla, but without balance they can't utilize the elements. Instead their magic becomes something twisted. Something that can't heal, that can only harm. Something that can burn, but not regenerate."

She crossed back to the couch and sat. "So what's the macro?"

At her question all of the amusement slid out of Francis's eyes. "The macro is the war."

SIX

"YOU'RE NOT GOING."

It was a flat statement and one that shot Daughtry's irritation factor straight up to ten thousand. She stood outside the door to her and Cody's quarters—not that he'd stayed there since Caroline had returned—and he stared at her, arms crossed, expression dark.

"We've talked about this—" she began.

His emotions slammed into her from across the bond. Frustration. Fear. But love? It was there, she told herself, she just couldn't feel it at that moment.

"I don't care if *you've* talked about it. It's unsafe and a bad idea," he said, his green eyes narrowed. "I won't let you go."

"Okay, He-Man," she began. If some small part of her had hoped that her leaving would spur Cody into action, then at least *that* piece of her personality was happy. It was the rest of her that was annoyed. "Bonded or not, you can't give me orders."

His lips had twitched at the He-Man reference before sliding firmly down into a frown as she had finished the sentence. "Why can't you—" He broke off and thrust a hand through his hair. "Why do you always have to be such a pain in the ass?"

Daughtry had to bite back her own frustrated words. "I'm just doing what I think is right."

He made a noise, an exasperated sound of disbelief.

"Say what you want. Register your complaints"—or, *hell*, do what he would have done just a few weeks before and go with her—"but I'm still going back."

His anger was a sharp whip against her mind, flaying it wide open.

"Fine. Get yourself killed," he snapped then turned and left. His pace and the heavy tread of his boots should have been loud. Instead his steps were silent on the floor as he went.

A perfect representation of what their relationship had become.

Silence and Cody constantly walking away from her.

"You could go a little easier on him, you know." John came up behind her, his shoulder bumping hers lightly.

"Seriously?" she muttered, wondering if she still looked like a pathetic, wounded puppy to her friend.

"He's having a rough go of it. Worried sick about Caroline, trying to track down how long she'd been held with the Dalshie and how much damage has been done. Now you're deciding to leave?" John shrugged. "It's not exactly the best time for you to go."

"It may not be the best time, but I have to go." It *had* to be now. With the weather cooling, with fall turning into full winter, she was running out of time to help Kaitlin and if she didn't fix the little girl's vision soon, it would be too late. The girl's fate was the last one Daughtry had botched and coming all too quickly. She'd thought that if she'd just interfered a little, just told Kaitlin to hold her mom's hand then the little girl wouldn't get hit by the truck.

But Daughtry had chosen wrong and her interference meant that Kaitlin was facing a brutal end at the hands of a murdering pedophile.

She couldn't let that happen.

John smiled. It was small. "I know you feel that way, sweetheart. But Cody's worried about you, you know?"

"Yeah." Worried, irritated, what was the difference?

He touched her cheek. "So you'll stay?"

"No." She had to try to undo the damage, not for her own sake, but for that of the little girl whose future she'd decimated. If what Francis said was true, then she had a shot.

She was going to take it.

And maybe . . . maybe there wasn't much left for her here. Cody was—

John nodded as though that was the answer he'd expected all along. "You got a ride set up? Cleared it with Dante? Protection?"

"I talked to him." Dante hadn't necessarily liked her decision to go back—what with her abilities barely more developed than a child's. But when she'd told him about her experience with the Dalshie during her kidnapping, how she'd found the two keys in his vision she could change, had mentioned that the person she wanted to save was an innocent little girl, his gray eyes had filled with sympathy. He'd given her permission to try, understood that the regret from her failures with the visions was eating at her, that she couldn't move forward until she shook off the barbs of the past. "He said he'd get me there and back." She paused, nibbled on her lip. "As for the protection, he said that if one of the guys wanted to use their time off then he'd approve it. Otherwise he couldn't spare it." Her eyes locked with John's, knowing that her expression was pleading and yet not knowing what else to do.

If she had to, she'd go alone. But she wasn't stupid. The Dalshie wanted her. It was smarter for her to have help, for someone to watch her back. "I was kind of hoping that you'd—"

"Oh no." His gaze lost any trace of softness, blue eyes hardening unnaturally. It was an expression she'd never seen on his face before—at least not until Caroline had returned to the Colony. Now the coldness with which John looked at her, the unexplained hostility—

She didn't understand the abrupt change and it was hard not to blame herself.

Nothing was different, but nothing was right either.

He shook his head and took a step back. "I'm not getting in the middle of this. Look, Dee. I understand why you want to go back, *really* I do. But this isn't the best time. The Dalshie want you and you're risking—"

"It's Kaitlin." The little girl's time was coming. And it was Daughtry's fault.

If she'd thought that would make a difference, it didn't. "It's still not the right—"

"I'll take you," Morgan's voice came from behind her shoulder.

Daughtry jumped, not having heard him approach. She turned and stared up at one third of the set of gorgeous triplet LexTals. "You will?" Morgan had been nice, but they hadn't exactly been painting each other's fingernails.

"It's not as if the Dalshie will expect you to go back to California." He shrugged. "What kind of idiot would leave the protection of the Colony?"

"Thanks," she muttered, trying to shake off the sting from the comments. Her desire to return wasn't about her. A little girl's life was in danger. Plus, it wasn't like the Colony was the be-all, end-all. She'd been kidnapped from right within its walls.

"You're welcome," Morgan said, either oblivious to her sarcasm or ignoring it.

Oblivious, she decided when he didn't follow up his response with anything snarky. "When can we leave?" she asked.

———

SHE HAD JUST FINISHED FILLING her small backpack when there was a knock on the door.

"It's open," she called, and zipped the bag closed.

"Ready?" Morgan asked as he came down the hall into the bedroom. He had a military-grade pack slung over his shoulder.

"Yes," she said before following him out into the hallway. They walked toward the Colony's front entrance. "Why did you agree to this?"

His hazel eyes went serious. "Besides the fact that I understand why you want to go back?"

"You don't," she said. It was an abrupt refusal that made him blink. But still—

How could he? He couldn't see the images running through her mind, couldn't grasp the violence broken down frame by frame, the easy way that innocent little girl's life had been snuffed out.

"Of course I understand," he said. "You have unfinished business with someone named Kaitlin. And because your line of work is manipulating death, I'm guessing it has to do with a vision gone wrong."

The matter of fact way he'd broken down the events which had been tormenting her for months made her feet slide to a stop.

He paused a few feet in front of her.

"Am I wrong?" he asked, turning back to stare at her.

Mute, she shook her head.

"Didn't think so." He started walking. "Come on." She trailed after him as he continued to speak. "I can see what you want to do, and I respect it. Wanting to atone, to fix a mistake—" He clamped his mouth shut, almost as if cutting off a burst of words he didn't want her to hear. His voice, when he spoke a moment later, was softer. "It's a good thing to do."

His words washed over her, made the numbness that had her soul in a stranglehold relax slightly.

They'd passed through the winding corridors of the living quarters and were moving into the common areas. Here the hallways widened and skylights were interspaced with crystal chandeliers. The murals—magic ingrained into the walls that helped power the Colony—were more tasteful, less DIY and more Monet. They were even boxed in with large gilt frames, giving the space a gallery-like feel.

Daughtry found that she preferred the amateur dabblings that decorated the halls of the personal quarters. Maybe they didn't belong in a museum, but they made her feel warm inside.

"What about the risk?" she asked when they entered the lobby. The marble floors squeaked under the rubber soles of her sneakers. "This isn't exactly the best time for me to be leaving."

She cursed mentally. Was she *trying* to convince Morgan not to come with her? His help was important and she needed someone to watch her back.

Still, she couldn't let him come unless he fully understood the risks.

"The Dalshie—" she continued.

He laughed. "You trying to warn me off?" he asked, then spoke before she could reply. "You don't have to tell me the risks twice. I have no desire to be Dalshie bait. But I'm assuming your reason for going now is important?"

She bit her lip then nodded.

"So we'll deal with things as they come."

"Simple as that?"

A smirk curled his mouth up at the corners. "Simple as that, sweetheart. Now can we get a move on?"

She nodded, but as she followed him across the lobby, it was hard to believe that it was that easy. That someone would help her just because she wanted to attempt to do the right thing. Why he even wanted to, when it seemed as though no one else —not even John, who'd always been there for in the past—cared.

And yet this wasn't the first time a LexTal had helped her. It wasn't even the first time she'd seen one go out of their way for another person beside herself.

Their sense of duty obliged them. They'd committed themselves to helping innocents, and while she wouldn't consider herself firmly in that category, she still shouldn't be entirely surprised that Morgan was willing to assist her in this.

Honor.

It was ingrained in the symbols of the LexTals' crest, the same marking that adorned the door of every one of the warriors' quarters.

Including the ones she shared with Cody.

What she needed to remember in this situation was that Morgan's help had nothing to do with her as a person.

She was a responsibility. Another duty to be taken care of.

Just like it was with Cody.

He was with her because of the bond, because he *had* to be. Because if he didn't foster their mental link, his magic would disappear.

No one knew how or why, but history said that bondmates didn't retain their powers unless they nurtured their relationship. Distance between them—physically, mentally—disrupted the bond, made it more susceptible to breaking.

And then they'd be human.

At her lowest point that was what she'd wanted. Now she wasn't sure. She wasn't getting visions as often—the bond shielded her—and while the worry that she would turn ate at her, Daughtry also couldn't help but hope that eventually her magic could be put to good use.

Maybe she'd be unsuccessful with visions, but could help other ways.

Plus, it wasn't as if it was a trial to be with Cody. Their powers were a perfect fit, their bodies drawn together like ants to a box of donuts, and the sense of homecoming when their minds interlinked was intoxicating. Of course that might just be Cody and not the bond. It was difficult for her to tell the difference. Was it merely instinct that drove her into his arms? Or because she cared deeply for the person he was?

She would have said both if not for the last two weeks.

Morgan pushed open the front doors and she followed him out onto the wide green space that made up the front of the Colony. The clearing was several hundred feet across and filled with a spider's web of gravel trails that led into the surrounding woods.

A soft splashing sound hinted at the small lake in the distance. She'd spent a good deal of time sitting on the shore, her bare feet dipped into cool turquoise water.

"Here," Morgan said, taking her backpack off from her shoulder. He pointed to a nearby bench and pulled out his phone. On the screen was a map of her hometown. "We need to appear somewhere secluded, away from where someone might see us. I can somewhat shield us, but it'll still look like we've appeared out of nowhere." He pointed to a park on the edge of town. "This is where I was thinking."

She shook her head. "It's far away from downtown, but its always crawling with high school kids ditching school. There's more of a chance of being spotted there than . . ." Her fingers dragged the map over, zoomed in, and then tapped the small nature preserve on the other side of town. "On the weekend this would be crowded, but a weekday like today and midmorning . . . we should be clear."

"Okay." He took the phone, his thumbs moving in rapid succession over the screen.

Daughtry waited patiently then not so much. She'd expected them to pick the location and then poof, be out of there.

Eventually, she asked, "What are you doing?"

He didn't even glance up. "This isn't a movie, Dee. My powers don't actually teleport us."

"Um." A pause as she tried to comprehend how they'd get to California if he couldn't actually teleport. "Then how exactly are we going to get there?"

"It'll be so fast that it'll feel like I've teleported us." He grinned at what must have been a confused expression on her face. "I can move air. Really, *really* fast. But I still need a location in my mind. Otherwise we could end up in the middle of the Pacific."

"But how do you know where to stop?"

"GPS."

"What, do you have one implanted in your brain?"

He chuckled, stood. "Sort of. If I see the location on a map or have the exact coordinates, I can get us there." He buffed his knuckles across his chest. "I'm a navigation system on steroids."

"Or a bird during winter migrations."

"I like my comparison better."

Men. She rolled her eyes. "I imagine you would."

He snorted, scooped up her backpack then wrapped an arm

around her. Her shoulders went stiff before she realized that he was pulling his magic.

The air shifted, bubbling, whirling around the two of them. "Just a shield," he said. "For oxygen. Or bird strikes."

"What—?" she started to ask.

But then there was a push of power, a blur of coloring, and they were moving.

SEVEN

DAUGHTRY GROANED as they slowed to a stop and Morgan released her.

She'd never felt nauseous on any theme park attraction in her life, but "teleportation" was some kind of ride. While they were actually in the air—flying past clouds and airplanes and the occasional flock of birds—it wasn't bad, almost like they were standing still.

The hard part was the take off and landing. There was a sudden push-pull as they gained speed, as though her brain was being jerked to the back of her skull. Not to mention her stomach. The sudden change in velocity was more than that organ wanted to deal with.

"Don't worry," Morgan said. "It gets easier."

Biting back the urge to tell him not to remind her of their return trip so soon after they'd landed, she sucked in a breath and said, "I hope so."

Her fingers massaged her temples for a few moments and when her head felt like it would stop spinning, she glanced around. It appeared Morgan had gotten them to their chosen location.

The weather was mild but with the slight crisp in the air that signified fall in Northern California. A squirrel chirped from its perch in one of the large oak trees and the gentle wind rustled the leaves. The small clearing that she and Morgan stood in was deserted, thankfully, the underbrush thick enough to provide cover.

"Ever run into one before?" she asked, pointing to one of the broad tree trunks.

Morgan looked up from where he'd been checking their packs. "Not yet." He laughed at the sound of incredulity she made. "Came close a few times as a kid though."

"You're not making me feel better." She took a few steps, found that her legs felt steady.

"Since when do you need to be coddled?" he asked, slinging his pack over his shoulder and handing her hers.

She paused as the question hit home. Was that what she was doing with Cody? Pushing him, begging for attention? She didn't think so, but Morgan's assertion paired with John's puppy comment didn't exactly make her feel good.

Maybe she *was* needy.

No, she thought after a moment. Now wasn't the time to start second-guessing everything about herself. Not when she was getting her spine back, not when she'd finally stopped with the self-loathing.

"I don't need coddling," she said, putting as much cool confidence into the words as possible. Damn if she'd revert back into the sniveling pile of goo she'd been before. Slinging her pack onto her shoulders, she turned away. "Let's go."

Morgan followed her down the trail, not speaking except to give her directions that would lead them out of the reserve. It was a nice walk, the cool wind blowing wisps of her hair off her face, the well-worn path grinding softly against her sneakers.

"What did I say that crawled up your butt and died?"

The question made her feet freeze for a second and she glanced over her shoulder. Morgan's hazel eyes seemed genuinely puzzled as to her mood. Damn. Why did she always have to take everything so personally?

After a moment she began moving again, the trees not quite as peaceful, the cool breeze not as refreshing.

Morgan didn't say anything further, didn't push her for an answer the way Cody would have.

Opposite techniques, but both extremely effective.

"I'm not weak," she finally said.

A pause. "I know."

Right. "Okay," she said and kept walking.

"So why are you pissed?" The confusion and frustration in his tone made her anger evaporate. He asked the question as if the entire female race was an organism he would never understand.

"I'm not."

He snorted.

"I'm not," she said again. "I'm tired of being mad and hurt and . . ." Her throat went suspiciously tight. She cleared it. "Anyway. I'm not pissed at you."

"Okaay." he said the word tentatively, as though he was afraid the next thing that came out of his mouth might set her off.

"I'm tough."

A beat of silence and she could practically feel Morgan's caution. "Yes?"

She laughed. "You might say that as though it were a statement and not a question, but thanks for agreeing."

"Anytime."

"Let's just keep moving," she said. "You can worry about the mysteries of the female population later."

Morgan's warm chuckle slid over her as they tromped through the woods.

THEY APPROACHED the house that had belonged to Daughtry's parents. Or at least the people who she'd believed had been her parents.

During her time in the Dalshie dungeon, Daughtry had found out that Daniel and Judith had actually been party to her kidnapping from the Rengalla when she'd been a child.

Kidnapping. It was kind of her thing.

Which shouldn't be funny, but the bad joke was also a welcome relief to the truth—that the people she'd believed to be her parents had actually been blackmailed to raise her as their own.

There hadn't been any love lost between them, but the few positive recollections she'd possessed were tarnished by the truth that had come out in the cell.

Love hadn't played into Daniel and Judith's relationship with her at all. She'd been a means to an end—and not the one they'd hoped for. They'd taken their own lives rather than stand and fight for her.

She'd been left alone. Again.

Which hurt more than it probably should have, now that Daughtry knew the truth. She'd only been a payday, not a daughter. A burden, not a responsibility willingly shouldered.

Theme of her life.

Shit. She struggled to shake off the memories. It was difficult to tuck away the feelings of disappointment, the slight tinge of betrayal. But it was time to focus.

The mansion Daniel and Judith had called home would be as good a place as any to start. With luck, she and Morgan could borrow a car or get some money to rent one. Dante had offered her cash, but she hadn't felt right about accepting it, and she didn't want to tire Morgan by teleporting all over town.

The protection and transportation that had come along with Morgan's presence, was something she was willing to accept. She wanted to be smart, to be safe. Money though? That felt different.

"Come on," she told Morgan as she led the way through a gap in the hedge.

"Wait," he said, stopping her with a touch on the shoulder. "Do you feel anything?"

Daughtry gave a mirthless smile. "You mean my built-in Dalshie detector?" For whatever reason—a quirk of her power or some weird instinct—she could sense when the enemy was near. Of course it presented itself as the creepy crawling sensation of bugs sliding under her skin and extreme nausea so that was fun. But it was pretty much the single useful thing she could do. "None as far as I can tell."

Morgan tilted his head in the direction of the house. "Let's move then. In and out only. This doesn't feel right to me."

She passed through the hedge and into . . . stillness.

The house was a tomb—a disturbed one at that.

Lawn chairs were overturned, grass was torn, windows were shattered. She and Morgan picked their way across the war zone that had once been immaculately groomed English-style grounds and Daughtry felt her gut clench.

Her childhood hadn't been easy, far from it. Her "parents" had expectations for her that were impossible for any adult to fulfill, let alone a child who didn't know all the intricacies of high society. Marry well. Be seen, not heard. Do not leave the house unless her appearance is perfect. Be a perfect hostess. No, scratch that, just be perfect.

It wasn't until she'd finally found the strength to distance herself from them that she began to understand how the constant criticism had weakened her.

She was a broken-down roof, patched up haphazardly instead of the entire leaking mess replaced.

It seemed impossible that she'd ever feel whole again.

That she would even know how.

Morgan pulled her behind him as they approached a French door that had more broken windowpanes than intact ones.

Part of her wanted to protest the masculine gesture, to prove she wasn't as broken as she felt. The rest of her wasn't dumb. *He* was the soldier. If he wanted to go first then she sure as hell wasn't going to stop him.

He reached around the shards of glass then unlocked and opened the door. As he stepped into the dim space, Daughtry couldn't help but gasp.

Ash was everywhere. On the furniture, on the windowsills, on the floor. It coated everything and made it difficult for her to breathe.

Morgan reached into his pack and handed her a mask. It had goggles and a filter. Once it was in place, she took a deep breath and was surprised at how well it worked.

"Good?" he asked, his voice muffled through his own mask.

She nodded.

"Stay close. I want to photograph this. Then we'll get the car."

Daughtry watched him pull out his phone and move around the room, snapping pictures from a variety of angles.

"What difference does it make?" she asked when he came close enough to hear her.

"Ever watch any of those crime shows?"

"Uh. Yes?" she said, wondering what the hell that had to do with anything.

"Think ash splatter instead of blood splatter."

Oh. "Do you really think someone can piece together what happened here?"

"Most, if not all of it."

Wondering why they would even bother with the effort, she trailed him around the first floor. Wasn't it good enough that the Dalshie had died? Why did they need to know where or how many?

But that thought was lost as she took in the damage. The scope of the destruction shocked her. Not one piece of marble wasn't cracked, not one wall unmarred. Paintings were torn down, holes torn in the furniture. It was almost as if the Dalshie had been looking for something—

"Where's the staff?" she asked. There had always been a few maids, the gardeners, a chef. If things had started exploding and magic flying, wouldn't they have run? Or called 911? Why hadn't the police come?

"I don't—" Morgan began as he pushed into the kitchen. His curse almost blistered her ears. She glanced over his shoulder and swallowed back a scream.

"Don't." His hands grabbed her arms, stilling her.

She hadn't even realized that she'd been trying to push past him until he grabbed her. "Don't," he said again. "Stop it, Dee. Don't look."

But she couldn't tear her eyes away.

They'd found the staff.

The bodies were more intact than most that she'd seen in her visions or during her time in the Dalshie dungeon. And yet it wasn't the blood coating the room that made her feel ill.

It was the horrified expressions on their faces. The fear in their eyes. She'd known the staff better than Daniel and Judith, and they were—

"I should have come back sooner. I—"

Morgan shoved her out of the doorway and pushed her

down until she sat on the floor with her back against the wall. "Stay there." He turned back to the kitchen, his phone out. He made quick work of the pictures, his normally tan skin pale by the time he emerged.

"Let's get what we need and get the hell out of here," he said.

"But what about—?" They couldn't just leave them.

"I know someone on the force. He'll take care of notifying the families." His voice went hoarse. "And getting them a proper burial."

"Okay." She blew out a breath then stood. Her legs were weak as hell.

"Where's your room?" Morgan asked as they climbed the spiral staircase. It creaked ominously under their weight.

"Last door on the right."

"And the safe?"

"Under the floorboards in the closet."

"You might want to wait here," he said as they reached the end of the hall.

With a shake of her head, she pushed open the door. "There's nothing that they could have done to it that would phase me. There's nothing in there that matters to me."

But when she saw inside the room, every drop of blood rushed from her brain, pooling into her extremities, into her weak-as-hell legs.

Because she'd been wrong. Very, very wrong.

EIGHT

IT WAS the size of the words that was truly horrifying.

Written in bright red letters that filled almost an entire wall, the message read:

WE ARE COMING. YOU WILL TURN.

It would have been better if the words had spelled out a threat to her life because becoming a heartless, soulless Dalshie was more frightening to her than death itself. When a Rengalla turned, everything good in them disappeared. The black magic took over, erasing all evidence of compassion, morality, any hint of softness. What remained was an empty shell with only the worst characteristics of humanity.

She swallowed, averted her eyes, and affected levity. "You'd think they could have used something less cliché than blood." There was no doubt the crimson liquid the words was blood. Besides the iron tinge in the air, Daughtry had seen enough of it to be certain.

Morgan didn't say anything. Perhaps he was shocked by her

choice of words, but minimizing the message made it easier to deal with.

She crossed the room, sidestepped the six-foot tall door hanging crooked by one hinge then stepped inside the closet.

A fireproof safe was hidden beneath one of the floorboards. *If* it was still there. "Do you have a knife?" she asked when Morgan poked his head in

He raised a brow, as if that were the most ridiculous question she'd ever asked, and pulled a blade out.

"Thanks." The razor-sharp tip easily slipped into the space between two boards. The wood separated with a *crack*, revealing a small keypad.

She hesitated. Though she had known the safe was there, she didn't actually know what was inside. Daniel had always stashed money around the house, and her hope was that the squirreling away had continued to this safe.

"Problem?" Morgan asked, peering over her shoulder at the keypad.

"Maybe," she answered truthfully. "I'm not sure what the code is."

"Did Daniel and Judith have an alarm system?"

"Yes." She frowned. "But what does that— *Oh*. You think it's the same?"

Morgan shrugged. "Worth a try, isn't it?"

Nodding, she input the four-digit code.

The safe opened with a *whoosh* and the tension that had gripped her gut so tightly relaxed, because there *was* money inside. She handed Morgan the thin stack of hundreds.

It wasn't until she was on her feet again that she realized the safe wasn't empty.

Frowning, she bent down, reached in, and pulled out a small diary. A rainbow unicorn was on the front and one of those cheap gold locks that little girls thought kept their secrets safe but in actuality, kept no one out.

Its surface was waxy, the picture on the cover familiar, and she could feel a memory on the edge of her consciousness, the first niggling sensation that something wasn't right, the coating of goose bumps down her arms.

"Uh, Morgan? We might have company—"

His hand was on hers in an instant and he yanked her close as his magic surrounded her. She barely had time to clutch the journal to her chest as he pulled her to the window.

Daughtry gave a little shriek and scrabbled at his arm as he started to toss her out the open window, but it may as well have been an iron band for as little success she had at moving it.

"What are you doing?"

"I can't safely teleport inside."

That was the only thing he said before he shoved her through.

The ground came up quick.

Grass. Dirt. Rocks. All faster than she could have imagined, each element of nature came into focus.

Oh, *fuck*. This was going to hurt.

She closed her eyes.

The crawling sensation beneath her skin increased.

Then instead of falling down, they began moving forward.

"Damn," Morgan said after they'd leveled out. "How did they find us so fast?"

Figuring that was a rhetorical question, she didn't answer. Not that she could anyway. Between the fall and the Dalshie, control of her nausea was tapped out. If she opened her mouth . . .

Well, it wouldn't be pretty.

They didn't speak until they were back at the reserve, shielded by the undergrowth and the thick stand of trees.

"You know, we have money at the Colony," Morgan said.

Yeah, she knew. But part of her had wanted to do this on her own—stolen pseudo-blood money, or not. Her parents had lived a life of luxury because of her, because of her biological parents' sacrifice. Didn't she deserve a slice of that?

The thoughts tore through her. Made her bones feel frozen solid.

Blood money? Wanting to get her slice out of life? *That* wasn't her.

But better that than the truth.

Because her real motivation was harder to face.

A part of Daughtry had *needed* to go back. To see for herself that all the betrayals were true, that her so-called parents had never really cared for her. That she was just a job, and one they hadn't wanted at that.

She'd wanted closure.

Instead, the pain was as fresh as the day she'd found out the truth about her upbringing.

It hurt too much. It shouldn't, because who cared if a pair of kidnappers didn't care about her? But that paired with all the crap going on with Cody made her feel vulnerable. Unlovable.

Pathetic.

A sigh escaped her lips.

Since Morgan was still staring at her, she forced herself to focus. "Yes," she said. "Next time I'll just take the money from Dante."

"Promise?"

Her lips twitched, the hurts receding as she concentrated on the present. "Scared?" she teased.

Morgan glared at her but amusement had darkened his hazel eyes. "Even I'm not egotistical enough to take on ten to one odds."

A nod. "Point taken," she said.

He grinned, and pointed to the journal. "What have you got there?"

Daughtry glanced down at the colorful cardboard cover. "Not a clue. I don't remember ever having a notebook like this, but it was below the money. I just—"

Her mind fumbled for a thought—a memory? Then it was gone. She shrugged, not completely understanding the compulsion that had made her bring the diary but trusting her instincts enough to go with it. "I think it's important."

He made a noise that sounded like agreement and nodded to the trees behind her. "We cracking that open now? Or are we messing with Oracle stuff?"

"Oracle stuff," she said and though she smiled, nerves made her hands tremble slightly. When she'd come up with the plan at the Colony, she'd tried to think through every outcome, had found a way to justify the visit to Daniel and Judith's home, even had an emergency exit strategy.

But now that she was about to actually mess with the visions, her heart pounded in her chest with the force of a locomotive, and her hands went clammy.

Could she really do this? What if she made it even worse?

"We'll get through it."

Her brows pulled together into a frown. "How—?"

"How'd I know you were second guessing yourself?" Morgan shrugged. "Dee, you're an open book." He'd been kneeling several feet away, checking their packs for the Nth time. Now he stood and crossed to her, fingers lightly brushing her cheek. "Want to talk about it?"

A shake of her head. The images of Kaitlin's murder were burned into her mind. That wasn't something she wanted to burden someone else with.

"Okay then." He pulled out his phone, glanced up at her expectantly. "Where to?"

"You have any juice left? The Dalshie messed up my car plans, but I have coordinates."

He crossed his arms, gave her a mock-glare. "All day, baby. I can go *all day*. And night. And—" He stopped at her laugh. "That's better." A pause, then, "Dante help you with that?"

"Yeah." Dante—despite being the oldest Rengalla that she knew of and having a fondness for paper and pen over iPads— had pulled off some Internet voodoo magic and managed to locate Kaitlin's address by hacking into the school district's servers and searching through their electronic copies of birth certificates.

Turned out there weren't that many Kaitlin's in the district and further narrowing by age had left her with only four families. Online satellite imagery had taken care of the rest.

Daughtry had seen Kaitlin's house in the vision, was able to pick it out of the line up of four. Which was lucky because the stress of three extra blind visits wasn't something she wanted.

Already she didn't know how the hell she was going to be able to pull Kaitlin's vision without coming off as a complete pedophile.

Here, let me touch your daughter. I need to do it so that I can save her life.

Yeah, that was going to go over well.

"Let me see," Morgan said as he grabbed the paper she'd pulled out of her backpack, and glanced at the fifteen numbers as if it made perfect sense, when to her it looked just like a list of . . . well, numbers.

He glanced up at her after a moment. "This the only stop?"

She nodded.

For now it was. If she managed to tempt fate and fix Kaitlin's future then she would figure out her next step, but her goal at this point was to stop one innocent little girl from being kidnapped and murdered.

"Okay." A pause. "Can I ask why here? Why now?"

The questions weren't unexpected and she knew that Morgan deserved the truth, even though the possibility of losing his support when he found out how badly she'd screwed up scared her.

"Yes," she said, and proceeded to explain how she'd accidentally pulled Kaitlin's vision while walking down the street several months before.

How she'd been unable to watch the little girl run from her mother straight into the street and get hit by a tractor-trailer. "I just couldn't stand by and not try," she said. "I thought that if I didn't mention the vision, didn't say that I had seen something—"

Her powers had been a mystery then. Daughtry hadn't known anything about keys or the risk of dark magic. As such, she had stumbled through trying to help Kaitlin and changed things, not for the better. Of course, *now* she knew why'd she'd made Kaitlin's outcome worse.

Her experience in the Dalshie dungeon had taught her something.

Kudos to her.

She'd chosen the wrong key. Instead of forcing Kaitlin to hold her mother's hand, she should have altered something else.

A cough cleared her tight throat.

"I tried," she said. "I screwed it up and Kaitlin is going suffer an even worse fate if I can't fix it." If she could pull Kaitlin's vision and search it for keys, if she could find a way to reverse it. If she could find some other peaceful end for the girl.

Morgan was quiet for a long time, staring not at Daughtry but at the surrounding foliage. His emotions radiated off him, big and impossible to completely contain.

But without a mental link to connect them—like the bond that held her to Cody—she couldn't discern them. Funny how this one time she would have liked to be in another person's mind, to be able to puzzle out the meanings of the expressions crossing Morgan's face. Instead she was normal, clueless.

Morgan might have been disgusted with her, or angry, or sympathetic. Or anything on the spectrum of emotions. And while she knew it shouldn't matter what he thought of her because Kaitlin was more important, Daughtry couldn't help but worry. If he left her now, the process was about to get a lot harder.

"I—" she began.

He met her gaze fully and the intensity in his eyes shocked her into taking a step back, but then he closed the distance between them and pulled her into his arms.

Aside from touching her cheek a moment before, he'd barely had contact with her. He'd held her during teleportation, of course, but that had been with an almost clinical detachment.

This was different. It wasn't sexual in any way. Instead, his arms wrapped around her were warmth, sympathy . . . friendship.

And as she sank into the strength that Morgan provided, blinked back the tears that stung her eyes, the loneliness that had been weighing on her eased.

"Thanks," she said, a few minutes later.

Morgan rubbed his thumb across her wet cheeks, wiping away the wet tracks. "Any time." He dropped his hands and nodded to the path.

Daughtry followed him and as he stepped under a leafy branch, his words drifted to her ears. "You're pretty amazing, Dee. Don't let anyone tell you differently."

NINE

IT WAS late afternoon before they caught a glimpse of Kaitlin.

She walked out her front door hand in hand with her mother. *Skipping*. Daughtry's throat clenched—a violent sensation that made it difficult for her to breathe.

"Her jeans have butterflies on them."

The words were gasped out. Rainbow freaking butterflies. And Daughtry had let the darkness taint her.

"I know," Morgan said. "But lock down those emotions. Now's the time to keep it together."

She nodded in agreement, swallowing hard, straightening her shoulders.

"You're right."

"Always am." He flashed her a grin. "We LexTals have a saying: Fight Now, Cry Later."

She looked at him in disbelief. "That can't actually be something that you say."

"True story." There was smirk on his face that made her unsure whether or not she could believe him, but before she could think on that too long, he was moving. "Let's go."

She stumbling after him, moving nowhere near as gracefully

as she rose from behind the bush and stepped out onto the sidewalk. Morgan reached for her hand and tugged her close, the better to keep with their ruse of a happy couple. They followed Kaitlin and her mother down the street, and Daughtry couldn't quiet the notion of déjà vu, having trailed the pair in the same fashion only a couple months before.

Hopefully the outcome wouldn't be the same.

"Good," Morgan murmured when Kaitlin entered a park, but tugged Daughtry's arm when she started to follow. "No. We need—" His gaze swiveled around a moment before stopping. He pointed to the ice cream shop on the corner. "*That.* Come on."

Two minutes later, they each had a cone in hand as they strolled into the park. "Here," Morgan said, and coaxed her down onto a bench very near where Kaitlin's mother split her gaze between her phone and her daughter playing.

"Play along," Morgan told her and then proceeded to wrap an arm around her shoulder. "She's watching so loosen up and follow my lead."

"What lead?" Daughtry asked through gritted teeth, feeling decidedly over her head.

"*This* one." He leaned in and pressed a kiss to her mouth, with closed lips but just a beat too long to be appropriate for a playground. Then he stood and swung her around in his arms. Her ice cream went flying. "Morgan!" she cried, clutching onto his shoulders.

It wasn't until he bent and placed his hand on her stomach with a tenderness that made her throat tight, that she finally caught on.

He glanced up at her, brows raised. Her lips curled up into a semblance of a smile and he caught up her hand, leading her back to the bench.

Daughtry felt almost violated at the scene, the easy falseness of the moment warping something she'd one day hoped to share with her future spouse.

With Cody.

The thought pressed on her lungs, made it difficult for her to breath. She swallowed against the emotions raging inside her and let Morgan pull her to his side. If that little bit of acting had put Kaitlin's mother at ease, if it allowed Daughtry to fix the vision, then it'd be a small price to pay.

"You could have at least waited until I finished my ice cream," she muttered, eyeing the smashed mess of what had been a perfectly acceptable scoop of double chocolate fudge.

"Noted for future false pregnancy reveals," he said. "Though if you'd eaten it faster—"

"Did your prince ask you to marry him?"

Both of their gazes swiveled around at the small voice.

Morgan recovered first.

"No," he said. "My wife just told me that she has a baby in her belly."

Their eyes rose at the sound of footsteps. "Kaitlin, don't bother them."

"Oh, it's okay. Your daughter?" Daughtry asked, trying to keep the conversation going.

The mother smiled. "Yes."

"How old?"

"Five . . . going on fifty."

They all laughed.

"Do you really have a baby in there?" Kaitlin eyed Daughtry's stomach with the unwavering scrutiny that only a very young child could pull off.

Daughtry nodded, unable to actually verbally agree to the statement.

"Congratulations," the mother said. "Let's leave them be, sweetheart."

"I want to do ten more slides."

"Okay."

"And then swings."

"Okay," her mother said again with a huff of laughter.

"Awesome. Use the twisty one, it looks fast." Morgan held up his hand for a high five, the light *smack* of skin on skin making Daughtry do the same. She slipped her fingers freed and reached out for her magic, allowing a faint purple sphere to gather in her palm.

Kaitlin's slap was harder than she would have expected.

That was the only cognizant thought she had.

The rest was instinct.

Her power grabbed at the bare skin of Kaitlin's hand and there was an almost sticky feeling as her magic surged forth.

How her gift of foresight worked was still mostly a mystery. The bond with Cody shielded her from unwanted visions, and with it in place she had to actively bring her magic into contact with another person's flesh in order to obtain visions. So while they no longer were accidental, how a touch was actually able to bring about the visions was something she still didn't understand. Why, of all of the Rengalla, did *she* have the ability? How did it connect with the tenets of Rengallan elemental magic?

Those were the questions she had no answers to.

And at that moment, she didn't care.

Because the fraction of a second of contact had been enough for her to pull Kaitlin's vision. She heard Morgan say goodbye to the pair, and more felt than saw herself rise to her feet, his arm secure under her elbow when she would have stumbled under the onslaught of images flashing through her mind.

She had replayed them in her mind, seen the man who would murder Kaitlin over and over in her nightmares, but actually feeling the vision, feeling Kaitlin's fear, the man's excitement—*that* was different.

The events in all their Technicolor goriness made it impossible to find distance.

She staggered as a wave of nausea surged and it was a struggle to slow the vision. If she was to locate the keys, she needed control, just like she'd had at the Dalshie dungeon.

Morgan managed to get her out of sight before she tossed her cookies.

Well, not so much cookies as that afternoon's protein bar.

Though in her current "state," puking wasn't all that odd. In fact, it added to their cover, she *was* supposed to be pregnant after all. Fuck. She shouldn't be thinking about that, about the lie they'd just told, or the fact that she'd hoped she and Cody would one day start a family. But her mind had latched onto any distraction in order to avoid revisiting the vision—

Foggy breath on a cold window. Chloroform. Knives. Blood.

She gagged again. But with a few deep breaths, she managed to cobble enough of herself together to reenter the vision. Scene by scene, she played the sepia-tinted images at a snail's pace through her mind. Could she do something with the window? An alarm system? But the faint golden sparkling that had been present on the "good" key in her vision at the Dalshie compound wasn't showing up anywhere on the window.

It was frustrating.

Her frame of the vision was limited to what the participants could see, so she couldn't discern anything more that the rear of the house and the two back bedrooms.

None of which showed any sign of a key.

Come on.

She played the images through to the end, forcing herself to sit through the graphic details as the man strangled and then dismembered Kaitlin's body.

But . . . there was nothing she could do. The road as he drove to the deserted warehouse was visible, but there weren't any cops she could alert, nothing she could manipulate on the car.

It wasn't like she could force him to drive into a light pole.

As far as she knew, the only two things she could manipulate were the keys.

And only *one* of those would end up with something positive for Kaitlin.

Retreating from the vision, she allowed the real world to seep back in. She was on her knees, her head hanging, breaths coming in gasps. Sweat poured down her face, dripped beneath her collar, and soaked her shirt.

"Are you sure you want—?"

She cut off Morgan's question with a terse shake of her head.

A beat of silence then, "Okay." He touched her shoulder and she flinched, too raw for contact. Just as quickly, his hand lifted. "Lean back," he told her. "There's a tree behind you. Rest for a moment."

The bark bit through her shirt, abrading her skin. "I don't understand," she said when she could speak again. "It's the same. I thought because I'd triggered the vision before I had my full powers that I was just missing something. But it's the same *damn* thing. I don't *see* anything."

"You said something about keys?" he asked the question tentatively, as if afraid it might push her past her breaking point.

That wasn't a stretch.

A sound of disgust crossed her lips—at herself, at the situation. "No. I can't find them," she said. "The guy goes into the bedroom and grabs her—"

She broke off as she realized that she'd never once looked at Kaitlin or the man. She'd beem focused on the circumstances, on the chain of horrific events.

Morgan sank down next to her, careful not to touch her. "What?"

"I-um." A shake of her head. "I think I've been going about this the wrong way." A tug pulled the vision to the front of her mind, and this time she focused on Kaitlin, saw the faint sparkling on the girl's mouth.

Yes! Daughtry could nudge Kaitlin with her powers, wake her up and her mother would come. It was such a simple solution.

So simple that she'd almost activated the key with her powers, actually had the globe of purple magic in the palm of her hand, ready to implant into the vision when she felt the niggling.

That little voice of caution turned her mind to the man.

The sparkling was centered on his pocket, on an envelope that had emerged when he'd removed the cloth soaked in chloroform.

There was writing on the envelope.

"Andrew Carpenter. 652 Laurel Lane," she gasped out and then opened her eyes. "*That's* the guy."

Morgan's eyes went wide. "Should we—?" He stopped, as if unsure how to finish the question.

Daughtry knew what he was thinking, because she was right there with him. If they could find Andrew, turn him over to the police, could they save Kaitlin? Could she trust her instincts in this?

"I don't know," she said then sucked in a breath, prepared to go back in. "Hold on."

Images passed through her brain.

It took effort to focus, but the envelope was marked, as was Kaitlin's mouth. They both looked like the other keys she'd been able to find.

Her mind was drawn to the slip of paper.

But it was also drawn to Kaitlin.

Wouldn't it be easier to trust in herself, her magic? If Kaitlin was awake, then her mother would be there and Andrew would run off.

What could she do with an address?

It was useless. Even if they managed to get it to the proper authorities, the police might not do anything, might not investigate a tip, might bungle the investigation.

There was no way she could trust—

Her eyes flew open and she looked at Morgan. "I know what I have to do."

TEN

VISIONS WEREN'T SIMPLE.

But by the time Daughtry and Morgan had finished searching Andrew Carpenter's place, they had a plan and she held a tentative amount of hope.

They'd found boxes and boxes of child pornography. Combined with the assortment of knives and freaky-ass journals, the evidence was overwhelming.

Morgan was pale but his gaze determined as he stared at her, phone in hand, waiting for her to make the final decision before he called his friend at the police station.

She bit her lip, and prayed to whatever deities were out there that she was doing the right thing. "Do it."

Morgan nodded and turned away as he talked.

A little while later a car pulled up. It was an unmarked sedan but not one of those boats that undercover police officers typically drove. A man got out and approached them.

"Do I want to ask?" he said to Morgan.

The officer was tall, well taller than her but smaller than Morgan and much lankier. He wore a smile but his gaze was hardened, as if he'd seen a lot of dark things.

She knew the feeling.

"No," Morgan said. "You definitely don't want to ask. But you need to get a warrant for this place. Say you got a report of suspicious activity or whatever. Just don't let that guy have his freedom."

The officer's lips pressed into a firm line. "That bad?"

"Worse."

"Okay." The officer nodded. "I'll take care of it."

"Thanks."

The man glanced at her, extended his hand. "Sorry, my job takes priority. I'm Sam."

"I understand," she said. "Please don't let us stop you from your work."

He inclined his head then walked back to his car, already pulling his phone from his pocket.

"Come on," Morgan said, pulling her away. "We'll watch from here."

Daughtry followed him across the street to where another building's courtyard faced the back of Andrew's apartment. She wanted to ask if he thought they were doing the right thing. Since it was a pointless question, she refrained. This was *her* mission, and blind reassurance wasn't going to make her feel better.

They sat in silence, backs against a tree and withered grass under their legs, as they watched Sam. He made a series of phone calls and soon another unmarked car pulled in. Then another.

The precision with which the officers worked was amazing. They'd established a perimeter without anyone noticing.

She definitely wouldn't have seen the casually dressed officers placed strategically around the building and street had she not been watching for it.

A different car pulled up, but this one Daughtry was intrin-

sically familiar with. Silver paint, beige interior, a stack of news-
papers on the floor of the passenger's seat.

Oh God. *Oh God—*

A warm hand grabbed hers. "It'll be okay."

She squeezed it hard. "You think so?"

"Don't doubt my instincts," he said. "They're flawless."

Her eyes rolled, but his words had done the trick. She was
able to watch the events unfold as, if not an impartial observer,
then at least in relative calm.

More than a dozen eyes followed Andrew's climb up to his
apartment. He ascended one flight of stairs. The next.

She held her breath as he opened his door but before he
could go inside Sam stopped him, showing him his badge, lips
moving.

Andrew shook his head. Backed away.

From her distance across the courtyard, she couldn't hear
anything, but the gestures made the conversation pretty clear.

Andrew's body language screamed guilt—he kept trying to
slink back into his apartment. Sam, on the other hand, was
unyielding. He positioned himself so that it was nearly impossible for Andrew to run.

But a moment later, Andrew did just that.

He didn't get more than two strides away before Sam
tackled him to the ground.

The rest of the officers poured up the stairs and into the
apartment. The noise should have been deafening, like the
cavalry riding in to save the day in an action flick. Guns blazing,
glass shattering, officers shouting. Instead, the whole process
was relatively calm and much quieter than she would have
expected.

More cars pulled in and the processing began. Flashes of
light—cameras, she supposed—showed through the apartment's

windows. Sam hauled Andrew down the stairs and into the back of a squad car.

After it had pulled away, presumably to take Andrew down to the police station, Sam came across the street.

He sat on the ground next to them and sighed. "I should say thanks for bringing that asshole to our attention." A long sigh. "But I'm more disgusted that he even exists in the first place."

His words made Daughtry wonder at her part in this. Had Andrew always been that way? A cruel, awful man who preyed on children? Or had her messing with Kaitlin's vision altered him? Drawn him to commit the awful acts?

Did she bear some of the responsibilities of Andrew's actions?

She knew that she couldn't control another person—that the boxes of photographs and journal were evidence of Andrew's intrinsic evilness. And yet, her powers gave her the ability to manipulate their deaths. If that wasn't control—

". . . bodies," Morgan said, drawing her focus. "But you need to be careful. When we were there . . ."

It took a bit for her to realize that he was filling Sam in on what they'd found at the mansion, then another few seconds before she was able to firmly push away the notion of her guilt to deal with later.

"I'll look into it." Sam turned at Daughtry. "Thanks."

Gratitude wasn't what she expected. Her eyes slid away, she shrugged.

He nudged her foot with his, and she glanced up. "I mean it. Because of you, we're going to be able to put that monster away for the rest of his life." He left, walking back across the court-yard to the crime scene.

As Daughtry sat there, her brain struggled to comprehend what she was seeing. What was working across the front of her mind.

It was a vision.

Kaitlin's vision. Cold fear swept over her. Would it—?

The images were familiar and different at the same time.

Because the tapestry of the vision was unwinding, separating into individual strands of color. Daughtry did her best not to panic. She knew this would happen. She'd changed something.

But what would the result be?

Slowly—*way too slowly*—the threads wound back together.

The vision began playing in her mind.

At first, she didn't understand it and when she reached the end, she had to force her mind to go back and replay it. Her throat tightened. Her eyes blurred. It took two more times through, before she began to believe it. Then she watched it again because it was so beautiful—if one could say death was such a thing.

But watching the elderly woman surrounded by a group of family and friends gently pass on *was* beautiful.

Love and compassion filled the room, drove every action.

And that made all of the difference.

"Daughtry?"

Morgan asked the question softly, as if afraid to break the spell.

Her eyes flew open and she launched herself at him. "We did it!" She pressed a kiss to his cheek. "*We did it!*" As his arms wrapped around her, pulling her in for a tight hug, she felt a niggling. A push in her mind.

It was anger, a hot, sharp slice of it.

She pulled back and glanced around, half expecting a group of Dalshie to have appeared out of thin air.

But it wasn't the Dalshie.

Daughtry forgot everything that had happened between her and the man who was ingrained into her very soul.

"Cody," she said, jumping to her feet and running towards him. "I did it. I fixed the—"

Her bondmate, the other half of her soul moved straight past her. He didn't look at her. Didn't touch her.

He strode up to Morgan and punched him in the jaw.

ELEVEN

"YOUR BOYFRIEND HAS a bitch of a right hook," Morgan muttered, rubbing his jaw. Despite the punch, he'd remained standing.

Daughtry watched Cody's retreating back. His shoulders were tense, his gait the forced smoothness of the critically enraged. *"Cody?"* It was a tentative brush of her mind against his.

"No." One word, two letters, and yet filled with so much hostility that she took a physical step back even though they only touched along the bond.

Her instincts told her to run and hide, to shrink from the pain.

The spine that she'd only recently found told her to fight.

She started after him only to be stopped by a hand on her arm.

"Maybe you should let him blow off some steam. He looks really pissed," Morgan said.

"He's not the only one," she muttered, pulling away from Morgan's grip and taking off after Cody again. It took her short legs a few blocks to catch up with his longer ones. But she had righteous fury on her side to fuel her strides.

She was tired of being unseen, of being a freaking doormat, of allowing herself to be hurt over and over again by the people she cared about.

No more.

He paused at a street corner and she did the same. About fifteen feet separated them but his presence in her mind was strong. He felt her—she could sense it—and yet he kept his back towards her.

Closing her eyes, she tried to find her calm, her center.

She'd chased Cody down and now had no idea what to say to him.

The sun was setting, sparse rays just peaking out over the top of the buildings on the opposite side of the street. The nearly black silhouettes looked ominous. A soft scuffing sound behind her almost made her jump out of her skin.

"Just me," Morgan said.

Cody started forward again. He turned down a narrow alley on their right.

She was tempted to turn around, to tell Morgan to take them back to the Colony. In the end, she decided that the quickest way to move forward was to get this confrontation over and done with.

Cody was waiting for them at the dead end of the narrow street. When he saw Morgan beside her, he growled.

Morgan put his hands up, a gesture of surrender even though his tone was hard as granite. "Hey dude, Dee and I are just friends. Don't get pissed at me because *you* left your girl-friend unprotected," he said. "I'll let that first punch slide, but the next time you take a swing at me, you're going down."

Cody took a step forward. "You fucker—"

"Stop." She put her hand against Cody's chest. He stopped, though he could have easily pushed past her. Her eyes turned to Morgan's. "Can you give us a second?"

He leaned in and kissed her on the cheek. Then whispered in her ear, "Kick his ass, Dee."

A huff of a laugh escaped her. "Not going to be a problem."

Morgan walked away and she rotated her stare to Cody. Crossing her arms, she narrowed her eyes—waiting for an explanation, or maybe for him to beg her forgiveness, or—

"Are you even going to say anything?" she demanded after a solid thirty seconds of silence.

He didn't answer and her mind drifted to the bond, testing, touching softly. When it reached his piece of the connection, the emerald strands of magic linking their brains, their souls, he recoiled.

"Don't," he said, moving away from her.

"Don't what?" she said and followed him. "Touch you?" She shoved his chest, brushed the green threads of his powers again. "Be *me*? Or maybe *love* you? What is it that you don't want?" Her questions had risen to a yell, probably drawing the attention of every single person in the neighborhood.

"You."

She froze, eyes locked on his, dread filling her stomach. "Me, what?" she whispered.

"I don't want *you*."

She inhaled a breath very, *very* carefully so that Cody didn't see just how much those words had sliced her open. He couldn't get clearer than that, could he? But then he kept speaking, and each statement was worse than the last.

"I don't want to be bonded. I never asked for this. I want to be free."

Anger made her retort, "You think *I* knew it was going to

happen? That *I* wanted the bond?" Tension was making her shoulders cramp, her jaw sore from clenching it so tightly.

His eyes darted away then back. One part of her thought the gesture was strange, that it wasn't like him to avoid eye contact. But then his words washed over her. "All I know is that when you showed up, everything got worse. It's all fucked up now. If I hadn't met you then I wouldn't have—"

"That's enough."

A hand settled on her shoulder, Morgan's.

She wanted to twist around and tell him to back off, to relieve the rage and hurt boiling inside her. But she didn't. Because her anger was directed elsewhere. On the man in front of her. At herself.

Her fingers found Morgan's hand and gave it a quick squeeze. Then she stepped forward, away from the comfort at her back and towards the man who she'd thought would be her future.

"This is about Caroline," she said.

Part of her still expected him to deny it. She wouldn't be able to find out the truth, didn't dare touch the bond again to ferret out the answer in his mind. Not when he'd recoiled so completely at the last brush of her consciousness against his.

But then he spoke. "*Of course*, it's about Caroline."

Her shoulders dropped an inch but she dutifully straightened them. She was strong, stronger than anyone knew. She didn't need this. "You think I had something to do with her abduction."

Cody's eyes flashed in irritation. At her.

No surprise there.

"Don't be ridiculous," he said. "You didn't have the capability. But you should have—"

That made her hurt fade and her anger burst. "*What, Cody?*

You've seen into my mind. You've seen every piece of my past," she said. "What should I have done?"

The silence that descended was thick and uncomfortable.

"I—" He broke off and shook his head, as if there was a thought deep inside of him that was trying to get free.

"Are you okay?" she asked, instinct had her mind reach for the bond, wanting to reassure herself he was okay, while her fingers extended toward his jaw

Two things happened at once. First, Cody went ramrod stiff, dodging her physical touch, and, second, she found her consciousness slammed up against an impenetrable brick wall. It shouldn't be possible, that barrier, but her mind couldn't get through. His angry mental voice shouting, *"No!"* in her brain had her freezing and halting any further attempts.

She didn't dare reach out to his mind again.

She was battered, mentally bruised and bloodied from their interaction.

"You—" he began again.

"Just go home," she murmured when he didn't finish the thought. Her footsteps were loud as she turned and walked out of the quiet alley, Morgan following her.

"Cowgirl?"

It was the tone more than the nickname that made her face him. "Yeah?"

"For what it's worth, I'm sorry."

She let out a mirthless laugh. "Cody, *I'm* sorry to say that your apology isn't worth shit."

"You okay?" Morgan asked her about ten minutes later.

"I always am." She shrugged. "And since you've allowed me

my ten minutes of sulking, let's talk about what we need to do next."

"Alright."

"Do we need to testify or anything with Sam?"

"Nope." Morgan tugged her arm to guide her around a pile of—yuck—*something* she didn't want to look too closely at. "And he's going to investigate your parent's house."

"Thank you," she said, and meant it. Their families deserved closure. Justice. But Daughtry thought that the LexTals would probably have to be the ones to deliver that.

"Hey Morgan?" she asked a minute later.

His eyes found hers. "Yeah?"

"I just wanted to say thanks for coming with me." His support had been a surprise, but a welcome one that had come when she'd felt abandoned by Cody. By John and Suz.

"Dee, I know we don't know each other well, but I meant what I said before. I respect what you're doing and who you are." He flashed her a smirk. "Even if I didn't, I would have still come. I'm a LexTal. It's my job to protect people."

"Even if they're being stupid?"

"Especially if they're being stupid."

She took that in, then, "For the record, do you think that's the case now?"

He laughed, full and outright, and she found herself chuckling alongside him.

"Since there's only one safe way to answer that question, I'll let you draw your own conclusions."

"So it's safe to say that you think I'm the smartest person in the history of the universe?"

"Yes. Exactly that."

She snorted and indicated the street. "This way. Since the police don't need a statement. I just want to make one more stop before we go home."

As they moved down the sidewalk, the shops got a little nicer. Still old, but well kept. The shoppers weren't in the nicest clothes and didn't carry the most expensive purses, but most of them had a ready smile available for her as she passed. *This* was why she'd chosen this neighborhood to live in. Older and run down, yes, but there was an intrinsic friendliness that enveloped the entire community.

Like snuggling into a cozy, oversized sweatshirt.

"Where are we going?" he asked, and it was less of a demand than simple curiosity.

"A bar." She smiled at his expression—bewilderment—and continued. "I want to talk to the bartender. She's a friend of mine."

"Oh. Okay."

"Yeah. And it's actually"—she pointed to the sign—"It's right here." She pushed open the door and walked across the scarred wood floor. The feeling that surrounded her wasn't exactly homecoming, but it was something close. This was the place where she'd found a bit of peace when she'd been at her lowest. Scanning the bar, disappointment flowed through her when she didn't see Darcy.

"Oh, she's not here." Daughtry paused. "We can just go. Maybe I can come back another—"

The swinging doors that kept the kitchen separate were pushed open and Darcy walked out.

"Darcy," Daughtry called, pushing towards the bar, lips curving.

Her friend looked up and a wide smile broke out over her face. "*Daughtry?* I was worried about you. You doing okay?" She reached forward, as if to hug her, then aborted the movement.

"I'm good," Daughtry said and leaned forward, pulling her friend into a quick embrace. "I'm really good actually." It was *mostly* true. This kind of innocent touch—simply hugging a friend—was something she would have never been able to do a few months before.

Darcy pulled back and studied her. "I think you are," she said after a few seconds.

Dee smiled, touched a lock of her friend's hair. "You changed it."

Darcy shrugged. "I decided that red wasn't my color."

"Well blonde sure is." *Combined with a body that would make a grown man cry.* "I bet your tips are great."

"That, at least, is true," Darcy said with a laugh. "So what—"

Daughtry glanced over her shoulder to see what had made Darcy stop talking. She waved to Morgan. "Come here," she told him. "This is my friend—"

"Darcy."

She glanced between them, taking in Darcy's pressed lips, her pale skin. "I'm guessing you two know each other?"

Silence.

Darcy spoke first. "You could say that."

"I *could* say that?" Morgan's tone went furious. "We *know* each other? Really? *That's* how you're going to play this?"

"I'm not playing anything I—"

A prickling feeling went up Daughtry's spine and the burning sensation of nausea crept up her throat.

"Um, guys?" Her stomach began to churn.

"You always—"

"*Me?* I—"

Daughtry whistled. Loudly. They both froze.

"We need to go," she told them. The nausea ramped up, and Daughtry's skin began to itch. The Dalshie were getting closer. "Like *now.*"

"What?" Morgan asked.

"Oh, Christ," Darcy said. "You always were an idiot." She

hopped over the bar, picked up a stool and chucked it at the glass window.

The bar wasn't crowded, but there had been a fair amount of noise covering their conversation. After the chair sailed through the pane of glass, absolute silence descended.

Darcy strode through the debris, not a care in the world. She kicked a fallen beer sign out of her way. "God, I've wanted to do that forever," she said. "Let's go, Dee . . . *Adonis*."

Morgan finally found his action.

He helped Daughtry over the wreckage and out onto the sidewalk.

"Maybe next time we could just use the door?" she asked.

Darcy laughed. "That place had it coming. Trust me." She looked at Morgan. "Teleport us out of here, pretty boy."

Morgan was already on it, pulling them down a nearby alley and wrapping them in his magic. He put an arm around each of them.

Daughtry waited for him to make some joke about leaving with one woman and then coming back with two. Because, *really*, this was the perfect time for a pithy comment about a *ménage a* something.

But Morgan didn't say anything.

The distraction would have helped, because her skin crawled, and bile burned the back of her throat.

A moment later, she was glad he hadn't delayed another second.

Because as they shot into the air, she saw the Dalshie. They strode into the alley, almost casual, as if they hadn't actually been pursuing them. Their creepy red eyes tracked them as they ascended.

One of them lifted his hand in a cheerful wave.

A shiver skated down her spine.

"Morgan?" she asked.

"I know," he said and increased their speed.

Soon the Dalshie were out of sight, but Daughtry couldn't shake the feeling that there were things happening she didn't understand.

She didn't like the feeling at all.

TWELVE

"WHY DIDN'T YOU TELL ME?" She demanded the moment Morgan had dropped the net of magic. They were on the front lawn of the Colony, the cool breeze and splash of the lake waters doing nothing to calm her.

Another person. Another betrayal.

Darcy glanced at Morgan who shrugged. The expression on his face was hard, and he raised an eyebrow as if to say, 'This is your problem, not mine.'

"Daughtry—"

Commotion had them all turning around. Caroline swept towards them, followed by Dante and John.

John put his hand on her shoulder, but she shook him off and stormed forward.

"Made a friend, did you?" Darcy asked, eyeing the pissed off redhead.

"Long story," Daughtry told her, and stepped in front of Morgan and Darcy. "Yes, Caroline?"

Cody's sister stopped in front of her, hand extended, green sparks of magic fluttering around her palms, gathering into crackling strands of emerald.

"Enough," Dante said and grabbed Caroline. "You're supposed to be resting. And you're not to use magic until we—"

"I'm not turning!" Caroline yelled at the top of her lungs. "I was beaten. Tortured. I was fucking burned but I *never* turned."

Silence descended.

"Um," Darcy whispered.

Daughtry ignored her, addressing John and Dante instead. "She's right. She hasn't used black magic." Dee trusted her instincts and they were telling her that while Caroline might hate her, might want to murder her, she hadn't gone over to the dark side.

Caroline's eyes flashed. "Don't you *dare* defend me—"

"You're sure?" Dante asked. His gray eyes were serious, his mouth pressed thin in displeasure. Whether at her or Caroline, Daughtry wasn't sure.

She answered anyway. "Yes, I'm sure."

"Okay." He glanced over Daughtry's shoulder. "Darcy, welcome back. Let's bring this discussion inside."

Caroline looked as though she wanted to protest but when Dante tugged on her elbow, she allowed him to escort her inside. Daughtry waited until they had moved off before stopping Darcy. Despite all of the animosity roaring off Caroline, that wasn't what had Daughtry upset.

"You're one of us?" she asked.

"Yes, I'm a telepath," Darcy said, her brown eyes were laced with guilt.

A small breath of air slipped past Daughtry's lips, the sound revealing way more of her hurt than she wanted. Her friend had been able to see what was going on in her mind and still hadn't said anything?

Darcy winced. "Hey, Dee. It's not like that—"

She put her hand up. "You knew."

Silence, then, "Yes, but—"

"You heard my thoughts?" She'd been a regular at Darcy's bar before she'd known she was Rengallan, during the lowest point of her life. Her visions had taken over her life, confusion and fear had reigned supreme and more than that, she had been questioning her sanity.

Being able to manipulate death without warning tended to do that to a girl.

"Yes," Darcy murmured.

Her throat tightened and she swallowed convulsively. "Okay then." Remarkably calm words considering the feelings tearing through her.

"Dee. It's complicated. I—"

"I want to say I understand." Fuck. She and Darcy had spent almost every evening together for a year and Daughtry had considered her a friend. Her *only* friend. That Darcy hadn't even once tried to tell her the truth about what was happening to her mind—

She closed her eyes, breath slipping slowly between her lips. "I can't talk about this right now."

"I—" Darcy stepped in front of her, expression regretful, but when the other woman reached forward as if to touch her shoulder, Daughtry stepped back.

Out of reach.

Those words seemed to describe so much of her life as of late.

"I really am sorry," Darcy told her, dropping her arm.

"I know." She pushed around her then paused, unable to burn one of the last bridges tethering her to this place. "Later, okay? We can . . . let's just talk later."

When the betrayal wasn't eating at her.

It was one thing to have missed the signs that she'd been struggling with powers she didn't understand. But to be a telepath, to see into her mind and know what was happening . . .

To not do anything. *That* was harder to accept.

"*Daughtry?*"

The gentle brush of Cody's mind almost made her jump out of her skin. And it felt so damned right that she wanted to curl into the comfort he offered, no matter that it was a drastic one-eighty from an hour before.

Nope. She'd reached her limit on martyrdom.

And yet she found herself wondering if it was weak or strong to ignore Cody.

"*I can hear your thoughts, you know.*"

Sighing, she sensed him reading her side of the bond and while her mind didn't recoil, exactly, from the touch of his consciousness, she definitely put some distance between them, used it to shore up the defenses around her heart and soul.

"*What do you want?*" she thought.

"*I—Are you okay? I felt that you were upset.*"

So many things went through her mind at his concern. Hurt, anger, frustration, and hope—damn her soft heart. "*I'm good.*"

"*Listen. I want—*"

"*Look,*" she thought, not particularly interested in hearing anything that he wanted. Not at that moment, not so soon after he'd hurt her. "*Thanks for your concern, but I'm fine.*"

"*Daughtry—*"

"*I need to go.*"

"*Cowgirl—*"

"*No,*" she thought. "*You don't get to call me that. You're hot then cold then hot again. I just can't stand it anymore.*" Her rage and anger were intertwined, twisted together in a sick mass of emotions. Abruptly, she calmed, the feelings fading as exhaustion ate at her. "*Stop tormenting me, Cody. Please, God, please just leave me alone.*"

Though she wasn't speaking aloud, her breaths were rapid, her heart pounding.

This was too much.

The entrance of the Colony was in sight and she could see Dante waiting for her. The urge to flee physically and mentally was strong, almost stifling—though she knew she could only successfully manage one of the two.

It took effort to pull back from the bond, to shove it into the farthest corner of her mind. But by the time she reached Dante, her consciousness was clear, the bond regulated into a dark corner where Cody would be unable to hurt her. At least that's what she hoped.

Dante's gray eyes were calm as she joined him. "Did it go well?" he asked.

For a second, she thought she meant with Cody, because that had been going about as well as an elephant in a china shop. But of course, he knew nothing of what was happening in her mind and the memory of Kaitlin's vision morphing itself into something peaceful, of playing some small part in removing an evil person from society was perfect the distraction to the sadness in her heart.

"Yes." She smiled, letting a little of the victory soak in. "It did."

"Good," he said simply. "Why don't you head to your quarters and rest? I'll have some food sent up."

The small kindness surprised her. She'd expected an inquisition, and though she'd had permission, also some chastisement for actually taking off. "Really?"

His lips turned up. "Really." He started for the hallway leading to the kitchens then stopped. "But we'll talk in the morning," he added in a tone that brokered no argument.

Great.

"And, Daughtry?"

She glanced up.

"Next time don't act so surprised when someone wants to take care of you. You're family."

Her heart squeezed tight at the sentiment. She'd heard the words before, but hadn't really believed them. It wasn't like her track record with family was great. Her bio parents murdered, her adopted ones not treating her like a paycheck or obligation rather than a daughter. Morgan's declaration of respect might have been the closest she'd come to actually thinking that it could be true, but part of her felt like the idea, the words were dangerous. After all, the notion been implied by Cody's actions and look how that had turned out.

It was probably a sad statement about her life that it affected her so strongly. But after a lifetime of feeling unworthy and unloved, the notion was heartbreaking. In a good way.

A few beats passed before she was able to manage a nod. Then she made her way to the hall that lead to her room. For once, Daughtry was thankful for the crisscrossing walkways and turns. What used to be so hard to navigate before she'd learned her way around had become a haven for her to avoid social interactions.

Her avoidance skills on point, she didn't have to talk to anyone on the way to her quarters, but when she stopped outside her room, there was something waiting for her.

A thing.

At least it wasn't a person.

Sitting on the floor just in front of her door was a small crystal vase with a single cut flower inside.

A violet. The purple matching her eyes exactly.

The tears she'd successfully held back before poured out.

She touched the spot on her chest, where a silver charm had once hung. All that was left of the necklace Cody had bought her months before was the brand-like scar. The charm had melted when her magic flared out of control, turning the pendant to ash. But the mark on her skin was identical to the bloom in the vase.

"Oh, Cody," she murmured, remembering the feel of his fingers on her nape as he'd placed the necklace around her throat, his whispered promise that it would allow him to always give her flowers.

The way love had poured through the bond, coating her heart in hope.

She pressed her hand to the lock panel and felt her magic sync with the Colony. Purple fibers crawled out of her palm and into the walls, combining with those from the rest of the Rengalla to run the compound.

The door to her quarters was calibrated to only her or Cody's powers, an apparently simple piece of magic with an explanation that had flown over her head when it had been told to her.

Click. The lock opened and she pushed inside.

Her fingers brushed the scar on her chest one more time as she sent up a small prayer—to fate or God or whatever forces were at work in the universe. But even as a small part of her wished for things to get better or easier, the larger piece of her knew that her life hadn't ever been that easy and that it never would be.

Still, as she showered and changed then answered the door to accept the tray Dante had sent up, she hoped.

Because just when she'd written Cody off, there was that small slice of faith. A sign the man she felt so much for wasn't totally lost. Her fingers grazed the velvet soft petals of the flower he'd given her, and she let herself hold on to that feeling.

Even though it was fragile and translucent and could be shattered with the softest puff of air.

THIRTEEN

"WHAT DO you mean *he's gone?*" Daughtry asked later that week. "How can someone just be *gone?*"

"He and Caroline left three days ago." Dante stared at her from across his massive desk. Multiple piles of paper were precariously perched along its wooden top. A pencil holder was jammed full and his laptop was covered with Post-Its.

But amongst all of the chaos, he sat like the calm leader he was, completely unfazed and totally comfortable whether it be with paperwork or hand-to-hand combat.

"Why?" Daughtry hadn't seen Cody since her return to the Colony, not a single sign of his presence since the violet, but she'd just figured he was giving her the space she'd wanted. That she hadn't sensed him leaving . . .

Well, *concerned* didn't begin to cover her emotions.

Stupid for wanting him to come to her, idiotic for waiting for him to make a move, and—

"He and Caroline wanted some privacy so they decided to stay at their family cabin."

"Cabin?" she asked, even though she was really thinking, *Family? Since when?*

Cody hadn't had much of one, biology aside. He'd been dumped off at an orphanage at the age of six because his parents had thought him a Null, or a Rengalla without powers. So it surprised her that there was a place belonging to his parents he actually wanted to visit.

"Yes," Dante said. "It's about four hundred miles to the North and fairly secluded. But the area is safe. We've got surveillance and alarm systems in place, with a safe room and even an emergency beacon."

A frown pulled together her brows. "So if you know where he is, why did you want to meet with me?" She hadn't talked with Dante since he'd debriefed her after her success with Kaitlin and the pursuit by the Dalshie.

"If there was the slightest hint of trouble, I'd have sent someone in to teleport them out."

Okay . . .

Some of the tension that had been knotting her stomach released. If Dante didn't think there was a problem—

"The issue is," he began, totally obliterating the relief she'd been feeling. "Cody *did* call for a teleport. But he told Morgan to return with Caroline because he'd left something behind. When Morgan returned for him, he was nowhere to be found."

She was starting to understand where this was going. "So you think that he *doesn't* want to be found?"

"Yes."

Irritation began to course through her.

Daughtry didn't want to leave the Colony again and definitely not because Cody was being stupid and running off like a child. Francis finally had time to tutor her and now that she'd had some success with the visions, had been able to use her magic without being overwhelmed by black magic, she wanted to learn about the rest of her powers.

Slowly, carefully.

If she chased after Cody that opportunity would be lost.

"Where's Caroline now?" It *had* to be asked. If Cody's sister was back at the Colony, Daughtry needed to watch her back, and if Caroline had decided to join the search, then Dee just might need body armor.

"Caroline returned to the cabin."

Obviously, Caroline had come to the same conclusion as her: Cody was pouting, going all stupid-brooding-male. And Dante wanted Daughtry to get him to come home.

No way was she about to—

She asked the question anyway.

"What would you like me to do about it?"

The corner of Dante's mouth turned up. "Bring him back, of course."

A sigh, her heart already knowing what her mind didn't want to admit. Regardless of the past weeks, Cody held too big of a chunk of her heart for her to simply let him go.

"What makes you think that I have any power over him?"

Dante shuffled through a stack of papers. "Daughtry, you're his bondmate. You have the ability to see into his mind and soul." He glanced up at her. "I'd call that power any day."

"How DO I get myself into these situations?" Daughtry muttered as she stood in a pair of arms that did nothing to her heart, her body.

Morgan tightened his grip, pulling her closer into his side. "Guilt, Dee. You've gotta let go of it. Though," he said with a small smile, "If guilt is going to drive you to kick Cody's ass then I'm all for it."

She sighed even though she felt a tinge of amusement.

Morgan was right. *If* Cody was pouting because she'd

finally stood up to him then she wouldn't just be kicking his butt, she'd be . . . well, *something* bad. Of all the stupid things to do. Going off and hiding? He was nearly a hundred years old and acting like a petulant child.

"What's the plan?" Morgan asked, drawing her out of her inner tirade. They were in the front of the Colony, getting ready to depart for the cabin.

"You take me there. I use the bond to find him. You teleport us both back."

Simple. Or it should be. Because the truth was that she was having a hard time feeling Cody at all. She tugged their connection out from the corner of her mind, did her best to focus on it, but the bond felt different. Almost as if it was stunted or being interfered with. Or—

Focus. This wasn't the time to worry about it, not seconds away from a teleport. If she couldn't find Cody once they arrived at the cabin *then* she'd panic.

They had never tested the outer limits of their connection. It was possible he was just too far for her to feel.

It might mean nothing.

It might mean *everything*.

But it wasn't like she'd been able to feel him when she'd returned home or sometimes even at the Colony before their estrangement, he'd been far enough away that she could barely sense him.

This felt different, though.

And now she was kicking herself for not reaching out to him sooner. That would have made her task a lot easier. But she hadn't been willing to brave the minefield of hostility and anger awaiting her on the opposite side of the bond.

She sighed again and turned to face Morgan, who was looking down at her, one brow raised, hazel eyes amused.

"Is this the point where you ask me why I'm doing this?" he asked.

There was a brief hesitation in her response, her taking a moment to wonder if she was really so transparent, or if he might have a touch of telepathy, before she nodded.

He rolled his eyes. "And then *I* have to reply that it's because of mutual respect and a well-developed sense of responsibility?"

"Um . . . yes?"

"Let's just skip all of that and I'll tell you the truth." He shot her a grin that would have fried more than a few brain cells if she'd been remotely attracted to him. "I'm nosy."

Her lips curved up to match his. "Like that old couple that peaks through the blinds and watches the neighborhood for delinquents?"

"Exactly."

She snorted. "You're—

"An idiot," he said on a huff of laughter before his arms tugged her close and squeezed. She melteed into the tight hug. "*And* you're beautiful when you smile," he murmured.

Uh-oh. The intimacy of their contact hit her and she pulled away. "Morgan—" she began, warning thick in her tone. If he thought—

He frowned down at her. "Where did you just go?" He reached for her again and she stepped back. "Dee?"

"I can't," she said, increasing the distance between them by a few feet and admitting the truth. "I love Cody."

His expression went confused. "Okaay . . . I know *that.* So what's going on? Did I hurt you?"

A shake of her head, her finger pointing between the pair of them. "I can't do this with you."

"Do *what?*"

She started to respond but then understanding dawned on his face, and he laughed, the jerk.

"You think, *me?*" he asked, laughter bubbling up. "With *you?*"

Her cheeks heated and she turned away. Fuck. Okay, so obviously she'd misread things, but he didn't have to make it sound like that. Maybe she wasn't in his league, but what was she supposed to think?

Compliments and contact didn't come without an ulterior motive.

"I'll be right back," she told him. "I forgot . . ." She didn't bother to expand on the lie, just let it trail off as she hurried away from him. The doors to the Colony slammed closed behind her.

Good, she'd just take a second—

Her feet skittered to a stop when she almost ran into Suz.

"Hey," she said carefully.

"Hi." The doctor's gaze slid away and she shifted as if to move around her.

Dee caught her arm. "You okay?"

"I'm fine," Suz replied, though her eyes wouldn't meet Daughtry's. "Just busy."

"Oh, okay," she said, releasing her. "I'll . . . uh . . . let you go. Did you want to watch a movie—"

"Can't." Suz took a step toward the doors. "I'm busy."

"I was going to say when later this week." Dee tilted her head to the front lawn. "I've got to do a couple of things with Morgan and Cody then meet up with Francis to practice my magic and—"

"So you *were* you faking it."

She looked up into coffee-colored eyes. "Faking *what?*"

"The darkness? Losing control? Were you going for the

sympathy card?" Suz flung the questions at Daughtry like shiny blades.

Barely, *just barely*, Dee avoided flinching back. Instead, she kept her voice quiet, though her head was spinning. Every time she had dealt with one antagonist, another appeared—usually in the form of someone whom she used to call friend. Apparently, she needed to work on her ability to read others because she was damned tired of the people chastising her being those she cared most about.

"How could you think that?" she asked. It was soft, though laced with steel. Didn't Suz understand at all?

Suz didn't respond, just stared at her, those chocolate brown eyes pinning her in place. She'd started working for Suz again that week, resuming her gophering duties, and while things weren't exactly the same as they had been before Caroline's return, they were getting better.

Or so Daughtry had thought.

Something froze inside of her at the sight Suz's frosty exterior.

Cody. John. Darcy. Suz. Every person she'd let herself trust.

They all just kept hurting her.

She turned away from her friend, from one of the first Rengalla to truly show her acceptance, who'd taught her to trust.

Clearly, she was a poor judge of character. Or maybe . . . her next thought hurt more than it should because it held a gem of truth.

Lightning didn't strike in the same spot over and over.

If people continued to turn on her, then perhaps it wasn't *their* fault. Perhaps . . . it was hers.

She started to walk away then spun to face Suz again. "You of all people should understand. I thought you were my friend. I thought—" She broke off when an odd expression came over the doctor's face. It was confusion with a dash of horror—wide eyes, mouth dropped open—but before she could ask if Suz was okay, the look was gone.

"You thought wrong." Terse, ice-filled words that managed to numb and wound Daughtry at the same time.

"Good to know," she said, then turned away and started walking, her desire to get away from Morgan's amusement and Suz's coldness morphing into a real destination.

Because though its inference hurt, Suz had a point.

The darkness in her mind *hadn't* made an appearance as of late and she'd had a relatively easy time controlling the vision of Kaitlin.

She wanted to think that meant she was cured. That maybe her selfless sacrifice at the Dalshie compound had rid herself of the near-overwhelming urge to destroy everything in sight when she used her powers.

Except . . . she didn't think it was that easy.

The tutoring sessions with Francis were a bad idea. She'd never be the innocent do-gooder she so desperately wanted to be. *No*, she was the grenade with the pin pulled. Each second brought her closer to the explosion.

If she could just put the pin back or throw the damn thing into the ocean, then everything would be okay.

She gave a perfunctory knock on the door in front of her and pushed inside.

Dante looked up. "Everything okay?"

"You offered money when I first came here. Is that still on the table?"

FOURTEEN

"READY?" Daughtry asked as she came back outside.

Morgan had plunked down onto the grass to wait. At her approach, he stood. "Hey, Dee. I just wanted to say—"

She put her hand up to stop him before smiling reluctantly. "I already know that what you said didn't mean anything. I'm over it, I swear."

It hardly compared to the other things that had been said.

"No." The word was fierce, a drastic alteration from his normal tone. "You *don't* understand." He tugged her hand, drew her in front of him.

"Morgan—"

"No, you'll listen to me. Or I swear to God, I'll—"

"What? Spank me like a child?" It felt good to get angry, to stand up for herself. Even if it was with the one person who hadn't betrayed her.

Not yet anyway.

"Yes. *Exactly* that." He rolled his eyes before he put his hands on her shoulders. "Look at me and *listen*. I'm not interested in you."

Her eyes were on his, staring into the mix of brown and

green and gold that made up his irises. At his words, she felt her cheeks go hot. "Reading that loud and clear," she muttered.

"Shut up," he said, the order not anywhere close to harsh. Instead, his voice was gentle. "You're so frigging beautiful that you're hard to look at sometimes."

Her jaw tightened and she shook her head.

"It's true. But it's not just the outside, Dee. It's your heart," he said. "You have this big heart. Full of honor and determination. And I hate that it's been so damn bruised." He squeezed her shoulders lightly and sighed. "But then I look past your heart and I see your spine. And *fuck*, I'm surprised it's not made out of iron. How you have so much strength shocks me."

She shook her head. "I don't feel strong."

"I know. And that's precisely why you are."

The swell of emotion receded as she tucked Morgan's words away into the private corner of her mind. The one that held her happier memories. It wasn't very full, which should have made her sad. Except that as she slipped his sentiment inside, it buoyed her.

It might be total bullshit, but it was still the nicest thing anyone had ever said to her.

She sucked in a breath and smiled at him. "Okay, Jeeves. Is my ride ready?"

He laughed as he tucked her backpack over his shoulder. "Anytime, Dee. You have your cell?"

She patted her back pocket. "Right here."

"Good. Then let's go. I've got a date tonight."

"You're a total sleaze."

"Don't I know it."

She laughed as they shot into the air then forward, the clouds and trees and birds whipping by faster than her eyes could track.

IT WAS FREEZING when Morgan dropped the shield around them. Icy wind whipped her ponytail over her shoulder and the ends snapped her eyes.

"Damn," Morgan said, noticing her jeans and T-shirt. "He didn't tell you to bring a jacket."

"No, that's okay," she said through clenched teeth. If she released them they would chatter like some weakling.

Morgan didn't reply. Just gave her a pointed look as he took his coat off and slung it around her shoulders. It fell almost to her knees and the arms were way too long, but she stopped him from rolling them up. At least that way they kept her hands warm.

"Here," he said, "I'll show you the cabin."

As he led her down the little track of worn grass, she snuggled into the warm leather jacket, noticing the scent was a mix of sweet and spicy. Almost like sunflowers and cayenne.

She smirked. Somehow it fit him. Even the girly, floral part. It tempered some of his wickedness.

"What are you laughing about?"

"Nothing."

"Hmm," he said, eyeing her. "Nope. Never mind. I don't want to know."

They walked in silence for a few minutes before Morgan pulled her to a stop. "Here we are."

The cabin was well lit and smoke came out the chimney. Lights flickered through the window, indicating a television was on.

That was when she smelled a rat.

She whirled around. "Seriously?"

Morgan raised an eyebrow, shrugged.

"Intervening old grannies," she grumbled

He grinned. "Told you so myself."

"Is Caroline even here?"

"Oh, the Wicked Witch of the West is here, alright. She just won't be for long."

Daughtry sighed because part of her wanted to pitch a fit and demand that Morgan take her home. She hesitated, considering if she could pull it off.

"Don't bother," he said. "Hysterics don't get to me." A beat. "Which is why I get to bring Satan's Princess home."

"I thought everyone liked her," she asked softly.

Morgan didn't say anything for a while, just matched her strides as they closed the distance to the cabin. "Everyone feels for her, that's true. But *like?* No. She burned too many bridges for that."

Dee frowned. "But that wasn't even her."

"Before that. It's not like she was a fucking ray of sunshine before she was kidnapped." He snorted. "She was a total bitch. Arrogant, snotty, too good for everyone else. A total nightmare. Why do you think no one recognized the change?"

"But Suz and John—"

"Do you think either one of them would have ever put up with her shit?"

"No, but—" Daughtry honestly didn't know what to say to that.

"She's a different person with them."

"And not with you?"

He rolled his eyes. "Different doesn't begin to cover it. She hates me."

"Why?"

Morgan flashed her a grin. "I may or may not have 'accidentally' set her hair on fire right before our finals for Primary. She had to wear a hat for her pictures." He crossed his hands over his heart and affected a sad expression. "It was tragic."

Daughtry chuckled. "I bet."

They went up the two steps to the front door and knocked. She didn't miss the slight protective movement Morgan made as he shifted his body so he was in front of her.

"She can't hurt me." That one shot had gotten through, but the shield had recalibrated. It would protect her from further strikes.

"Not with magic she can't," Morgan agreed. "But I wouldn't put it past her to use cutlery."

Daughtry shuddered, easily remembering the rage that had made Caroline's green eyes molten. She couldn't disagree, wouldn't put it past the other woman to pull a knife. "Why does she hate me so much?" she asked.

It was a question she'd thought about often and one she didn't have an easy answer for.

Was Caroline jealous of her relationship with Cody? Did she just dislike anyone new entering the family? Did—

"I hate you because you look exactly like the bitch who tortured me."

FIFTEEN

DAUGHTRY AND MORGAN WHIRLED AROUND, both taken aback by Caroline's silent approach.

"LexTal?" Daughtry muttered under her breath.

Morgan gave a chagrined shrug. "She's sneaky."

Caroline glared at Morgan. "You."

He gave a mock bow. "Your chariot awaits."

"I'm not leaving."

Morgan just smiled and it was the first unfriendly one that Daughtry had seen. He looked as though he would like nothing more than to hog-tie Caroline and then drag her home.

But instead of doing that, he pulled a paper out of his pocket and handed it over.

Caroline read the slip of paper then grunted in disgust. "I'll get my things."

"No," Morgan said and when Daughtry looked up in surprise, he addressed her instead of Caroline. "Sneaky, remember? She'd probably lock us out and bar the door."

"That was one time!" Caroline said, outrage in every syllable. "And I was eight."

"You were ten," he retorted. "And Daughtry isn't the bitch who took you."

The silence descended on them like a tidal wave, devastating and powerful.

"I know that," Caroline finally said.

"I don't think you do." It was Daughtry who spoke the words and she was almost surprised that they'd come from her. She'd been so freaking weak lately, standing back and letting everyone walk all over her.

"I don't hate you." Cheap talk from Cody's sister.

Daughtry rolled her eyes. "Could have fooled me."

"It's just that"—Caroline's voice faltered—"You're so much like her."

Fuck. Daughtry didn't want to have any sympathy for the other woman, but it was filling her to the brim anyway. She'd experienced only a small portion of what Caroline had been through, and still bore the soul-deep scars.

"Have you lost your fucking mind?"

The sentence exploded out of Morgan.

But he wasn't done.

"How dare you even insinuate that? Daughtry isn't one of them," he said. "She's the strongest person I know." His eyes narrowed on Caroline. "The *strongest*."

Caroline stepped forward to stab her finger into Morgan's chest. "I don't *know* anything about her. And I can't be bothered to find out. Cody's already left her, so she can't be worth the trouble."

"You're insane," Morgan said.

"That might be the singular thing I am not," Caroline said, stepping back and dropping to the top step of the porch. "I'm broken, I'm scarred, I'm a complete and total bitch, but I am *not* crazy."

"You—"

Daughtry was touched that Morgan was standing up for her, but she was also beyond tired of someone else taking care of her problems, sick to death of people talking about her like she wasn't there.

"Time to go," she told him.

Morgan and Caroline broke off their argument and stared at her.

She gestured to the sky. "I think you two can continue this discussion in the air."

Morgan nodded, face calm despite the concern in his eyes.

"I won't—" Caroline began.

"Shut up," Morgan said. "Let's move. Daughtry, call me when you've found him."

"Will do."

"Or if you need help."

A shrug. "Of course."

"You'll turn." Daughtry's gaze flashed up, saw that Caroline had focused on her. "They *always* turn."

She didn't bother to acknowledge the words, just turned away to study the cabin and deliberately ignored the icicles that popped up in her blood at Caroline's statement.

The little house was smaller than she would have expected, less stacked logs and more country cottage. Small windows dotted the sides, and were framed by dark green shutters. The porch wrapped around the exterior, so close to the surrounding forest that pine needles dotted the wooden deck and railing. Despite her attempts to ignore Caroline's words, despite the loveliness of the cabin, a sick feeling crept into Daughtry's stomach. She knew the accusation was just that—a baseless claim— but having her deepest, darkest fear thrown so casually into her face made Daughtry sick.

"Are you all right?" Morgan asked from behind her, the question quiet, almost whispered into her ear.

"I'm fine!" Or she would be once he and Caroline left. She wanted to cry or punch something. But she *needed* to think. And damn, now she was being awful to the only person who cared what happened to her.

Friend of the year award.

A deep breath loosened her lungs and she turned to Morgan to apologize.

He shook his head, expression understanding. "I'll go. But you'll call me if you need anything?" He tipped up her chin, forced her to look at him.

"I won't need anything."

"I know," he said, his tone rueful. "You're okay."

She gave a weak smile in return. "Always am."

He gave her upper arms a light squeeze before he faced Caroline.

"Ready?" he asked.

Caroline stepped towards Morgan then paused, her mouth opening.

Daughtry cursed under her breath. If Caroline said something else, she'd—

"The key's under the flower pot." She tried to ignore the trace of regret in Caroline's voice. The woman obviously didn't mean it.

Morgan wrapped his arms around Caroline. "Try not to enjoy the ride too much, princess."

"Go fuck yourself."

"Anatomically impossible but I appreciate the creativity."

Caroline's retort was lost to the air.

Daughtry started toward the planter, but couldn't focus. Her emotions were out of control and her heart practically tore a hole in her rib cage trying to escape.

Instead of unlocking the cabin's door, she ran.

Trees caught on her hair, branches cut at her cheeks as she

pushed through the thick forest. But nothing mattered except . . . space. She needed five minutes without anguish, five minutes to just be with herself, to not worry about bondmates or dark magic.

To be herself without anyone judging.

It wasn't until a gust of wind blew under Morgan's jacket that she paused, chest heaving, knees wobbling. She gripped a tree for balance and sucked in air. She wasn't the woman who'd taken Caroline, she knew that. But the image she'd seen through Cody's mind, the woman's cruel smile and cold eyes, was like looking into a mirror that reflected the worst in her.

Because no matter how many times she tried to convince herself that the female Dalshie was just wearing a glamour—using it to try and create dissension amongst the Rengalla, trying to torment *her*—Daughtry couldn't shake the feeling that she'd been looking at a glimpse of her future self.

Fuck. She punched the tree.

The bark abraded her knuckles and the thick trunk hurt her a hell of a lot more than she it. "Shit!" She waved her hand in the air, knuckles stinging, bones burning. That had been beyond stupid.

Turning, gripping her injured hand in her other, she turned back for the cabin.

And promptly tripped.

She landed hard, a gasp of air escaping her lungs as the hard ground knocked the wind out of her. Tears streamed down her cheeks as she struggled to catch her breath, but after a moment, she managed to get some air into her lungs and find her feet.

Hands stinging, she glanced around the forest, trying to remember the way from which she had come. It was early afternoon, night still a good chunk of time away. But if she didn't get moving, get back to the cabin—

She had no clue what kinds of animals were in these woods,

just knew she sure as hell didn't want to find out. Dee had no desire to be prey to predators of the animal or Dalshie variety. Plus, her luck was just bad enough that a mountain lion could appear at any moment. Or maybe a bear.

After waiting a beat, half-expecting the sentiment to come true, she sighed and returned her attention to the remembering the path out of the trees.

When nothing caught her attention, she reached into her pocket for her cell.

She'd call Morgan and—

"Shit." The screen was cracked and black. She pushed every button on the damn thing, praying that it might magically start working. But no, it was dead. She was lost and didn't know the way out and . . . she'd been an idiot to go off in the woods by herself.

Cursing her stupidity, she picked the direction she thought she'd come from and began walking.

Almost ten minutes in, she inhaled, the smell of burning logs wafting up to her nose. "Thank God."

The cabin was close.

Picking up her pace, lured by the idea of a crackling fire to warm her numb limbs, she hurried forward. Pretty soon sweat trickled behind her ears and down her forehead. She wiped away the stinging drops and paused for a breath.

It was hot. Almost scorching.

The realization hit her as abruptly as a car hitting a brick wall. A second later, she was whirling in the opposite direction and sprinting away as fast she could.

The air was dry, brittle. Smoke poured out of the woods. Twigs snapped and leaves crunched as animals joined in her exodus.

"*Oof.*" She hit the ground hard for a second time when a deer burst out of the brush and startled her. Her lungs burned, her eyes stung. She didn't know which way to run, not with so much smoke and heat surrounding her.

A pair of arms grabbed her. She launched herself into his grip, recognizing the mind then the pine and salty ocean scent as Cody's.

"What are you doing?" he shouted, his face furious and his skin an unearthly orange from the approaching flames. "Why don't you use your magic?"

Her jaw dropped open. "Maybe because I don't know how?" She stabbed him in his chest with her finger and he leaned back. "Maybe because I'm not sure if can use my damn magic without almost blowing up everyone in the vicinity. How's that for a reason? That good enough for you?" She shook off his arms. "Now if you're done yelling at me, I'd like to get the fuck out of the burning forest!"

She went to push past him and almost collapsed, having used up all of her oxygen yelling at him. Black splotches blurred her vision and she clamped her teeth together to keep from puking.

"Dammit," he snarled, scooping her up and sprinting away from the fire. He muttered under his breath the entire time, but she ignored him.

Yes, she was pissed at him. Yes, she felt like an idiot for not even considering using her magic.

But yes, she was grateful to be in his arms.

Stupid that he made her feel safe, but she was glad to relinquish the mantle of control. At least for a few minutes.

So she pretended not to hear his grumbling and instead closed her eyes.

His long stride was fluid, unyielding. They moved rapidly through the forest.

But not fast enough.

It seemed to get even hotter, the air drier, until every breath felt like the insides of her lungs were burned to a crisp.

She opened her eyes and saw that Cody's jaw was clenched. His shirt was soaked with sweat, soot had stained his blond hair a murky brown color.

He glanced down at her, eyes bright with worry. "Almost there."

She bit back the obvious question. It didn't *look* like they were anywhere. At least not anywhere that wouldn't end up with them as ashes. But a second later she was on the ground, frigid water soaking through her clothes, protest burning her throat and lungs like a hot poker. "What—?"

His body landed on top of hers, his gaze pinned her in place. "Trust me."

"I—" she started to say.

Then the fire closed in.

SIXTEEN

THE JOY in Cody's expression as his magic surrounded them took Daughtry's breath away.

His powers formed a dome of translucent green, liquid in its movements and clear as glass, but hard as diamonds when she touched it.

It was beautiful.

The space around them darkened eerily, and smoke crept in —black as a Dalshie's stained fingers.

The only sounds were those of their respective breathing, the squish of her clothing against the muddy riverbank below her. Cody's shield cast an odd glow on their skin and she had the uncomfortable feeling that this was what it would be like in Hell.

Except she wasn't with the devil.

Or was she? She glanced up at the man pressed so closely against her. Hard where she was soft, beautiful and sexy, he was certainly tempting enough. Add in the scar and the cruel way he'd treated her and—

Now she was acting insane.

The fire came then and every one of her thoughts poofed

right out of existence. She could feel the flames pounding against the shield, hear the crackling and roaring of the flames. It was deafening after the silence of the smoke.

Cody's magic was the only thing between her and certain death. If the shield failed . . . the notion made her a little sick.

But the magic didn't fail.

It protected them, muting the heat, the destruction of the fire. Their safety didn't come without cost, however, and she felt the strain in Cody's muscles, saw his hand shake as he wiped sweat out of his eyes. It was tough to watch him hold the shield in place—watch him struggle and not come to his aid. If she'd had an idea of what to do she might have. But she had no clue and in the end, figuring it out wasn't required.

The flames began to die down, the noise quieting, the smoke clearing.

Cody's triumph and relief collided with her mind as he relaxed on top of her. He rubbed his nose softly against the curve of her neck, inhaling.

Allowing the contact to sweep her away, she melted, softening further, allowing the hard press of him to sink into her body.

"Daughtry," he murmured, almost in trance. "I feel—"

That was when reality intruded. Because she wasn't "cowgirl" anymore, she was Daughtry. The woman he maybe wanted to have sex with, but not the one he wanted to be bound to. Not the woman he wanted to love.

She turned her head away.

Cody pushed back, an abrupt movement that had him bumping into the still-intact shield. He rubbed a hand over his face, desire warring with frustration, then let out a breath. The *pop* resonated through the air—a shift in the atmosphere as he let the magic go. The translucent green broke into its individual emerald strands, and faded away into the space around them.

Silence stretched across the riverbank. Daughtry said the first thing that came to mind, "That shield was amazing."

Cody shrugged. "We're lucky it worked at all," he muttered.

She coughed, lungs tightening painfully. "What do you mean?"

He sat back on his heels. "Are you okay?"

Another cough, but this time she nodded instead of talking. It hurt less.

The urge to reach across the bond and examine his mind was strong. She resisted it only because she could sense the direction of his concern. It was strong enough to drift over the no-man's land between them.

"What's going on with your magic?" she thought.

"Speak up," he muttered. "I can barely hear you."

Daughtry frowned. She'd been using her "normal" mental voice. Why couldn't he hear her?

"What's wrong with your magic?" she asked aloud.

"Nothing," he said.

She gritted her teeth, stifled another cough, and pushed to standing.

He didn't have any problems with directions, and it took less than a half hour for them to emerge from the forest. But by the time she saw the smoke from the cabin, a little trickle floating up into the sky that signified the cozy fire she'd been hoping for earlier, she was barely standing.

Black curled on the edges of her vision, her lungs were so tight that she could barely suck in a breath.

Cody took her arm then he unlocked the front door. He pushed his way in, led her across the empty space, and set her down on a couch that took up most of the front room.

She couldn't even stifle the coughs now. They were coming almost as rapidly as her breaths and each a lesson in burning, stinging pain. He moved away—into the kitchen—and she scanned the rest of the space, trying to slow her breathing, trying to distract herself by taking in the cabin. It was cozy and warm in a way she wouldn't have expected from a house that belonged Cody's frigid family.

A bed was shoved towards one side of the large room. Opposite that was a single door—which she hoped led to a bathroom.

The furnishings were expensive but sparse, a coffee table, a floor lamp, a woven rug. Just the necessities. Which she found surprising since the Colony was filled with luxury after luxury.

Cody came back into the room.

In his hand he held a knife. On his face was a pissed-off expression.

Daughtry gulped, and shrank back.

He rolled his eyes but his voice was gentle. "I'm not going to hurt you."

She wasn't so sure about that.

With the knife glinting in the firelight, she remembered his hostility, the anger in his actions as he'd so effectively pushed her away. Though he probably *wasn't* talking about hurting her feelings. For whatever it was worth, she'd always trusted Cody to keep her body safe.

Her heart had been the only casualty.

He sat on the coffee table facing her and gripped her wrist, tugging her arm toward his lap. "Hold still." Then he sliced at the leather jacket covering her arm.

She gasped, which started her coughing again. "Why'd—"

He nodded at the jacket and she followed his gaze, saw that the leather was singed, sticking to portions of her reddened skin.

His fingers probed lightly, sending bolts of pain through her body. "It might need healing." A tilt of his head toward her torso. "Your lungs and throat too."

"Mmmhmm," she said through gritted teeth and clenched

lips. She'd figured that part out already. A few deep breaths helped to unclench her mouth. "You'll heal it?"

He nodded, though she thought his expression looked worried. And when she dared to touch the bond, it was so muddied and tangled that she couldn't get a good read on his emotions.

So she waited, the throbbing pain in her chest feeling very much like a heartbeat. It wasn't easing, the nausea was intense, and her nerve endings were on fire.

"Cody?" she asked.

He sighed, extended his hands.

Green sparks should have emerged, coalesced into strands of magic that would surround her torso and end her agony.

Except nothing happened.

With a curse, Cody helped her lay back onto the couch. Then he leaned over her again.

For a moment she thought something was happening, that the connection in their minds sensed his magic. But as quickly as that feeling came on, it was gone.

He stood and stormed to the other side of the room, hands on his hips as he looked out the window, his chest heaving.

"What's going on?" she asked, levering herself up onto her elbows.

He turned. "I can't."

"Can't? Or won't?" She coughed violently.

"Dammit!"

She jumped, a gasp of pain escaping her lips.

"I *can't*." He paused before crossing back over to her.

"But the shield in the forest . . ."

"Dumb luck," he said. "Look at the bond."

"I just did. It's all tangled."

"No," he said. "Don't just glance at it. Feel it. *Look* at it."

Nodding, she let her mind slide along their connection, to

what had once been a beautiful symmetric web of their inter-twined magic. It wasn't woven now. Instead, it was tangled, rows of haphazard knots of purple and green.

What she hadn't noticed before were the breakages.

Violet and emerald strands were severed, standing separate.

Her eyes flew open. "It's—"

Cody knelt before her. "It's dying, Daughtry. I know you're mad, disappointed. But you *have* to forgive me. I need my powers—"

Something occurred to her then and it took a moment for her to absorb the shockwave of her own realization.

"Why did you come after me?" she asked.

He frowned. "I care about you. The fire. I didn't want you hurt."

"No. I mean why did you follow me when I was trying to save Kaitlin?" He hadn't cared when she left.

Please let it be because he was worried about her. Or even that he was jealous. Not because of his—

"It was your powers, right?" she asked when he didn't answer. Her gaze dropped, studying the faint pattern on the couch. "Your magic isn't working, and you knew that you had to make nice with me for the bond to work, for you to be whole." Her heart slammed against her ribs, breaths shallow and ineffec-tive, and *still* Cody didn't answer. "If you were so worried about your magic, then why did you leave without a word? The distance couldn't have been good for the bond."

"I—Caroline—"

"Of course. *Caroline.* You should have pushed your hand after the violet, Cody. I was ready to forgive you then." She sighed. "Can I use your phone?"

He reached into his pocket and held it out. "Cowgirl—"

"Daughtry, please."

Her fingers grasped the cell and moved furiously across the screen as she sent out a text.

"Daughtry," he began again. "It's not like you think."

"Cody," she said, fatigue settling over her like a thousand-pound weight, "I *know* it's *exactly* like I think."

SEVENTEEN

MORGAN AND SUZ showed up about two minutes after she'd texted.

"Dee, are you okay?" Morgan called, barely a foot into the cabin. The concern in his tone warmed her, helped her break through the ice around her heart. When he spotted her on the couch, he strode over to her.

Suz remained by the door, small black bag in hand.

Morgan grimaced as his gaze traced down her body. "Here." He set her backpack onto the floor with a *thunk*. "It was on the porch." A pause. "What happened?"

"Forest fires are a bitch," she managed through her raspy throat.

"Shit." He turned to Cody. "Why don't you heal her?"

"I can't," Cody ground out.

"Can't? Or won't?" Morgan asked.

Given that she'd asked the same question not ten minutes before, Daughtry couldn't help but laugh—then groaned when the action burned her lungs.

"Can't," Cody said between gritted teeth. He shoved Morgan back. "Do you think I want to see her in pain?"

"I don't know, man," Morgan said, standing upright and holding his ground. "You haven't exactly been sparing her it."

The two men locked gazes for a long moment before Suz spoke. "Give me some room," she said, walking over and squatting next to the couch. But when she glanced at Dee, she sighed, the barest smile tilting her lips. "Another injury?"

Sarcasm was a better response than tears in this case. "Told you I have skills."

"Apparently." Suz's eyes clouded as she assessed Daughtry's lungs, poking and prodding with her magic enough to make Daughtry gasp. Eventually, she sat back on her heels and said, "Your lungs are damaged."

Seriously? "Uh, yeah."

Suz shook her head. Sighed again. "Hold still."

Dee nodded.

Strands of brown emerged from Suz's palms. They wound their way around Daughtry's torso, almost scorching in the intensity of their power. Her skin itched and burned, and for a moment she thought she might scream her pain ramped up so rapidly. But by then the hurt was fading, and she could almost picture her lungs healing, the fluids leaving her swollen tissue as they returned back into their rightful places.

When the magic faded, her chest was slightly tender, but she could breathe fully.

"They'll be tender for a while so no big cardio plans."

"Okay." The doctor looked up. "Thanks."

Suz smiled and it might have been the first genuine one that Daughtry had seen in weeks. "I'd say anytime, but then I think you might take that to mean you could injure yourself again."

"Be right back," Morgan said when Suz waved goodbye and walked out of the cabin.

Once he'd gone Cody turned to her. "You didn't have to call him."

"I think I did." Uninjured she could handle anything Cody dished out. Hurt, both emotionally and physically, and she wasn't ashamed to want someone in her corner.

"Why is it that you always have a man around helping you?" Cody asked. "John and Tyler. Now Morgan. Why are you so goddamned irresistible to them?"

She absorbed the words with all the impact of a drive-by shooting, the sentences battering into her like bullets through glass, through metal, wood. For all the difference in strength between the materials, the shots still penetrated.

Even though she'd promised herself that she wouldn't allow Cody to hurt her again, the accusation still wounded.

Not that she would let him see that.

"So the implication then is that I'm completely *resistible* to you?" She sighed. Wounded wasn't the right word. She was numb.

"I—"

"I don't know," she said, cutting him off. "Maybe these people help me because I'm pathetic. Or maybe it's just because they have a sense of duty and responsibility that drives them to help others. A sense that you've lost when it comes to me."

Emerald eyes bored into her. "I saved you from the fucking fire."

"Yes, you did." She sucked in a breath. "Thank you."

"I'm not looking for gratitude. I want—I feel . . ." He trailed off.

"What?"

"Wrong." His fist came down onto the coffee table and she jumped. "Something isn't—" He shook his head.

Daughtry waited for him to continue and when he didn't, she let the silence stand. She was just too exhausted, too emotionally strung out to force the answers from him.

Sitting up, she reached for her pack, for the spare set of clothes inside.

Her movements were cautious, but she made it to the door across the room. When it proved to be the bathroom, she shut herself inside to change. There were two doors inside, one leading to a linen closet, the other to a separate bedroom.

Reaching into the stall, she started the shower then stripped out of her smoke-stained jeans and Morgan's jacket. She still felt weak, so it took some effort to get under the hot water, to wash the grime and ash from her body and hair. The clothes from her pack were simple—a T-shirt, jeans, a light sweatshirt. She slipped them on and then went to pull Morgan's coat back over the top, but her hand went right through the ruined sleeve.

Damn. Apparently, she owed Morgan a new him a new leather jacket.

When she emerged from the bathroom Cody was standing —arms crossed, shoulders stiff, back against the wall, his gaze pointed straight out the window. He didn't move when she bent and set her pack on the coffee table.

"Daughtry—"

It shouldn't have surprised her that he spoke, but it did.

But then again, she should have known better. *Of course* he wouldn't let anything go.

"Cody," she said, cutting him off. "I don't want to talk about it."

What could she say? That she was done being hurt, that she wondered where in the hell the man she'd fallen in love with had disappeared to?

That she almost wanted to let the bond wither and die completely so that she'd lose her powers.

Her life would be easier without her abilities.

She was damned tired of dealing with death and pain.

But before she could say any of that, Morgan walked through the front door.

"Ready?" Morgan asked her.

"Take Cody first," she said. "I forgot a couple of things in the bathroom."

"I don't—" Morgan began.

"It's not safe—" Cody said.

"It'll be for five minutes," she said. "By the time you're back, I'll be all packed up."

"I—"

"Go, Morgan," she said and into the silence sent him a pleading look. "Please." It was a whispered plea.

It worked.

He grumbled something about *déjà vu*, fixed her with a firm glare, and made her promise not to leave the cabin.

When she nodded in response, he grabbed Cody's arm and led him out the open door.

Daughtry followed them to the window, watching as they floated into the air and then disappeared from sight.

The moment they were gone, she sank to the floor, her head in her hands, her emotions like jagged shards of glass. Cody was . . . he wanted his magic more than he wanted her.

It hurt. *God* it hurt so damned much and yet . . . it didn't. It was as if a small part of her always knew that this might happen.

That she'd be an obligation, a burden that no one wanted.

Sighing and wiping her eyes, she pushed to her feet and crossed to the bathroom. She stashed her hairbrush that she left on the counter in her backpack, shouldered it, then opened the front door.

There was a decision to be made about her and Cody, about her powers and his, but right now she just wanted to soak in the fresh air.

Besides, Morgan would be coming back in a minute. She might as well wait there for him.

On the porch, she bent to retrieve the key from the flower pot then turned to lock the front door.

Distracted by the sticky lock, she didn't see the blow coming.

She heard more than felt the *crack* of something hard against her skull.

The ground came up to meet her face.

EIGHTEEN

"I TOLD you not to hit her so hard."

The voice slammed into Daughtry, a Mack truck of sensation that made her ears ring and her eyes water. With a groan, she attempted to bring her hands up to shield her ears, only to find her arms were secured behind her back.

"See. She's not dead."

"Shh," she pleaded, the pounding in her head intensifying.

She carefully opened one eyelid and then quickly closed it. Light was *not* a good idea.

"What happened?" she asked in the softest whisper she could manage. That volume level was all she could handle.

"Um. Well . . ."

The pain was fading slightly and with that came awareness of what they had said. She tried her eyes again, found that they didn't hurt nearly as much. "You hit me? Why?"

She took in the two guilty teenagers. Both were tall and lanky, with dark hair and baggy clothes. They were clean in a way that said they'd showered some time in the last week, but not the way that said they were particularly fastidious in their grooming habits.

Typical juvenile boys and since her inner Dalshie detector wasn't screaming at her, she guessed they were safe.

Or relatively so, given the head injury.

"Why?" she asked again, fixing them with her best glare. A jolt of surprise moved through her when it actually worked. They looked at each other and caved.

"Seth made us do it," said the one who was slightly taller.

"Who's Seth?" she asked.

"Um. I really can't say," the same boy answered.

Okay that wasn't going to get her anywhere. What she needed was time, and an opportunity to escape. To do that she needed to get them talking.

"What are your names?" she asked, glancing around. Trees surrounded her, and sounds from the road drifted to her ears, so she couldn't have been unconscious for too long. If she had to guess, she'd think they'd brought her onto the flat portion of the forest, the one that ran parallel to the road, instead of down the steep hillside.

A cove of pines surrounded the small clearing where she sat, a well-worn path weaving amongst the trunks easy to spot.

She shifted and they jumped like they'd been shocked.

"Don't move," the shorter one said.

"I'm not going anywhere," she said. "But can I sit up? My back is killing me."

Poor choice of words, she thought but managed to prop herself against a tree trunk when the taller one nodded. "So," she said. "What are your names? Mine is Daughtry."

"Yeah. We know. I'm Stephen." He pointed to his friend. "This is Eric."

Still digesting the fact that they knew her name, she forced a smile. "Nice to meet you," she murmured.

They grunted out some approximation of a response, a sign

that they'd had parents who'd cared at least a little bit about manners, before silence fell.

She waited a few minutes but when they said and did nothing further, she spoke. "Could you help me up? I need to use the bathroom."

The boys looked at each other with true horror and she bit back a smile.

A second later, Eric's face hardened. "Don't ask us to untie your hands because we won't. We're too smart to fall for stupid tricks."

Barely resisting rolling her eyes, she said, "Of course, I wouldn't ask that." Her tone was sweet as sugar, almost cloying in pleasantness. "But I will need help getting my pants off." Their eyes widened. *Not a deterrent*, she thought rapidly before an idea occurred to her. She smiled at the boys. "I just need you to get my tampon out of my pocket and—"

The rope was off her wrists and she was shoved into the forest before she could say more.

She waited until the boys had retreated a fair distance then slipped into the underbrush.

Sprinting, she moved parallel to the path and hoped to God that she was going in the right direction. The smoke was still behind her, so at least she knew that she wasn't about to run headfirst into the fire.

There was a yell and she paused. This was stupid. She didn't know where she was going, didn't have any supplies or survival skills to speak off. It was a real possibility that she could die out here.

The sounds of pursuit were getting louder so Daughtry did the only thing that she could think off.

She climbed a tree.

Yeah. Literally.

And it was a hell of a lot harder as an adult than it had been when she was a kid, but she managed to get a leg up over a branch and stash herself in the canopy of the pine tree.

The path was below her and a blurry line that she thought was the road wove through the forest in the opposite direction of where she'd been headed.

Eric and Stephen walked directly beneath her.

Fuck. Holding perfectly still, she waited for them to pass. Then waited some more in case they doubled back.

Her plan—what little of it that she had—was to head in the direction of what she thought was the road. Periodically she'd stop and climb another tree to check her progress. That way she wouldn't get lost. Maybe. Hopefully.

It was easier to descend the tree than it had been to get up and less than a minute later she was on her way. As she walked —still parallel to the path and not directly on it—she took stock of her supplies. She had a bundle of cash—Dante had given it to her back at the Colony without a protest. Thankfully, she'd tucked into her front pocket at the cabin. Now she separated it into three stashes, putting one in her bra, one in her sock, and the rest back into her pocket.

Then she climbed another tree. The spindly line that streaked through the forest appeared closer. It had better be a road.

Daughtry got back down without further injury, though she thought that this probably wasn't what Suz had in mind with taking it easy on her lungs.

By the third tree she could barely lift her arms to climb it.

Her hands and arms were cut, and a rogue branch had even torn a hole in her jeans. The grunge rocker look didn't work well when it was only one hole. It also didn't work with pink polka dot underwear. But then again there wasn't anyone to see. Muttering a curse, she slid down the last few feet of the tree trunk before brushing her sore hands gingerly on her jeans.

When she straightened, she looked directly into the eyes of a man.

Taller than her by a least a foot and with cold black eyes, he was frightening. But then his lips quirked and she noticed how lush they were. Suddenly he wasn't quite as menacing.

"Don't let me stop you," he said and pointed in the direction she'd been heading. "You seem to be doing fine yourself."

Daughtry didn't say anything, just moved past him slowly. He was giving off major alpha vibes, a coiled snake ready to strike.

Still, he didn't stop her as she continued on.

She was just disappearing behind a tree when she heard him chuckle. "Nice polka dots."

DAUGHTRY WAS TIRED. So tired that her feet had stopped aching a few miles before. Which wasn't a good thing because they were numb and that meant she kept stumbling.

Having reached her quota of injuries for the day, she bent, hands on her knees, and took a short break, trying to get her second—no, *tenth* wind.

But a few minutes turned into longer and by the time she found the mental fortitude to go on, it was difficult to force herself to her feet.

A warm hand caught her arm when she stumbled. "Easy," said the deep voice.

Part of her remembered whom it belonged to even as the rest of her was already reacting. Her self-defense training over the past few months meant the muscle memory was there.

Good for her. Unfortunate for the man at her back.

There was a crunching sound as her elbow connected.

"Fuck!" he yelled, voice muffled as his hands covered his face. "Why did you do that?"

"You surprised me."

"You broke my nose because I startled you?" he asked. "What's next? Castration because I commented on your ass?"

She rolled her eyes, her tiredness pushed aside by the adrenaline running through her system. "I won't apologize." But she touched his arm. "Here. Let me see."

"No."

A sigh escaped her. "Come on now. Don't be a baby."

With a grumble, the man dropped his hands. She grimaced.

"Okay," she said, taking in the already-forming bruise across the man's nose, the dark circles beneath his eyes. "Maybe I *should* apologize. How did I manage to hit you in the face?" Even now she had to stand on her tiptoes to see the injury.

"You looked like you were going to fall," he gritted out. "I was bending over. And don't apologize for protecting yourself. Here." He thrust his pack at her. "Grab me the towel."

She reached inside then started to place it in his open hand.

What she saw on his open palm made her scramble back.

Dark stains began in the center and radiated outwards, creeping across his skin to trail up his arms.

She turned in the opposite direction and ran as fast as she could.

NINETEEN

A HARD BODY slammed Daughtry to the ground, knocking the wind out of her, pinning her in place.

She struggled. The man was a Dalshie. Why hadn't she sensed him?

Her arms flailed, her legs kicked. For all the good the struggle did her. She was face first on the forest floor with a mouthful of pine needles and leaves. The last time a Dalshie had held her like this, he'd tried—

She didn't want to think about that. Her fear was palpable enough, squeezing her lungs, making it difficult to breathe, making her movements jerky and ineffective.

Strong hands manacled her arms then flipped her. The man sat on her stomach, his legs straddled on either side of her hips.

"If you touch me—" It took a breath for her to gather her courage when her voice broke. "If you lay a hand on me, I will kill you."

Her magic was just out of reach. As anxiety coursed, she fumbled with it, tried futilely to pull it closer.

The man's next words pulled her back into reality.

"You can see them?" he asked. "You couldn't before."

The words were filled with such wonder that she paused. The absence of malice, of taunting—the usual modus operandi of the Dalshie—made her hesitate. That and the fact that she wasn't nauseous, that her nerves weren't prickling. Her body didn't react like the man perched atop her was the enemy.

"I'm not one of them," he said.

She shook her head, unable to believe him. The stains marring his palms and arms weren't tattoos. They stained his skin, crawled up his arms, disappearing beneath the sleeves of his T-shirt.

"I'm *not* a Dalshie."

"I–I can't." She shook her head, swallowed hard. "Your arms. Your *palms*."

The man cursed as he got off her. He whipped around, punched the nearest tree.

When he thrust the bleeding fist in her face, the tang of iron was the only scent that filled her nostrils.

"What?" Her eyes were frozen open as she watched the blood drip from his skin. A trick. It *had* to be a trick. "Why isn't it healing?"

His words were filled with frustration. "Because I'm not a fucking Dalshie."

She scooted back a few inches, coming up against a tree. The bark was rough below her fingers, brittle enough that several pieces broke off and fell to the ground.

"Then . . ." A pause as she worked to swallow her terror. "What are you?"

"Forgotten."

The word meant something to her, something that tickled at the edge of her conscience.

"You're like Daniel and Judith," she said, realizing that she'd met Forgotten before, had seen markings like this on beings that weren't Dalshie.

A memory of the only father she'd known slicing his wrists, deciding to bleed out on the ground rather than fight, coursed through her. Daniel had been devastated by the death of his biological son and she . . . well, she hadn't been enough.

"Yes. We knew Judith and Daniel. We hid them for several years," he said. "We also knew *you*, Daughtry. Until they left. We thought you'd been captured and turned."

"No," she said, her voice a whisper.

Well, she hadn't turned yet anyway.

"Where are they?"

"Dead."

The man's brows drew together, his lips pressed into a firm line. He didn't seem surprised by the fact, just disappointed. "I'm sorry."

"Yeah."

It wasn't much of an answer, but she was glad when the man didn't push her on it. Because though they were gone, Daughtry still wasn't sure how she felt about the people who'd raised her. They'd been complicit in her kidnapping, kept her from the Rengalla, from a potential home, from a place she could have belonged.

Yet they'd provided her with food and shelter and when the money was good, everything material a kid could want.

Daniel had even given her a few happy memories—there'd been a fishing trip once, just the two of them, and he'd occasionally taken her to the movies.

But love had been in short supply. Especially from Judith.

Not that she could blame her. Because of Daughtry, their son Thomas had been taken and eventually killed.

That didn't exactly support maternal affection.

"What's your name?" she asked.

"Dominic."

"Can you help me get out of here?"

"Seemed like you were doing fine on your own."

Daughtry looked down at the myriad of cuts, the way her clothes were filled with tears. "This looks like fine?"

Dominic grinned. "Should I give the sleazy answer? Or the honest one?"

"Honest." She released a breath, her voice getting a little rough. "Always the honest answer."

There was a beat of silence before he spoke. "I saw Eric and Stephen sneaking around, decided to follow them. I was about to question them when I saw you scale that tree."

"You know them?"

"Yes." He gave a little smile. "But who really knows teenagers?"

"So you've been following me this whole time?"

"Well, they certainly weren't. They were tracking you in the wrong direction. And . . ." For the first time while she'd been talking to him Dominic looked slightly uncomfortable. "You looked scared."

"I'm fine."

"I'm not so sure you are." He continued before she could protest that. "Why were you with Eric and Stephen?"

"I wasn't with them on purpose," she muttered.

"You get lost?"

She shifted from foot to foot, not liking that she'd been taken so easily. Why had she gone out of the cabin? She'd promised Morgan. "Um. Not exactly."

"Oh my God," Dominic said, the words bursting out. "Tell me they *didn't*."

"Didn't what?" she asked, but he was already turning away, cursing under his breath.

She decided to take advantage of his distraction and slip back into the forest. The road had to be close. But before her first toe crossed out of the clearing Dominic spoke. "Don't go. It's getting dark and we have bears."

Bears? The thought made her freeze long enough for him to catch up to her.

"Come back to the Lodge with me. I'll get you a warm dinner and a soft bed. In the morning you can be back on your way."

She was about to protest. But it *was* getting dark. Already her eyes were having a hard time discerning the wilderness around them.

If Dominic was telling the truth about the bears—

She couldn't even be sure that she was headed the right direction. Not to mention remember the last time she'd eaten.

"What's the catch?" she asked.

His face twisted, a scowl deepening his features, making them seem almost harsh. "No catch." A shrug. "Okay, I guess there's one."

Her brows lifted in skepticism.

"You have to listen."

Some of the tension that had filled her faded. "I can listen."

DAUGHTRY KNEW she was probably stupid to go off with Dominic but the potential for being bear bait outweighed her other concerns.

If it had been lighter, if she'd been closer to the road or in more familiar territory then she might have refused. But as it was, her instincts said she could trust Dominic and so she followed him through the trees, his steps unwavering despite the fact that the sun had slipped completely behind the mountains.

"Watch it."

She stopped then glanced down and saw the branch directly in her path. "Thanks," she murmured, stepping carefully over it.

They moved at a decent pace, fast enough that they were making progress, but not so speedy that she felt like she was going to pass out. After her various experiments with tree climbing, she could appreciate the distinction.

"Are you really Forgotten?"

Dominic glanced over his shoulder and raised a brow.

"Fine," she said, having known the truth before asking the question. He "felt" like Judith and Daniel. "So you're one of them."

"Yes," he said, then kept moving.

Daughtry followed because—despite the bears—she was curious. The possibility that she could find out more about the Dalshie's experiments conducted on the Forgotten encouraged her. Judith and Daniel—and presumably the rest of the Forgotten—had been tortured during WWII, at the concentration camp Ravensbrück.

Before her time in the Dalshie dungeon, the Rengalla had thought that the prisoners of the camp had all been murdered, that the Dalshie had been unsuccessful in their attempts to inject magic into normal humans.

At least until Daniel had told Daughtry different, until he'd proved he could do magic—right before he ended his own life.

The Forgotten existed.

She just wasn't sure if they were friend or foe.

Dominic led her through the forest, a seemingly endless maze of tree after tree, without hesitation.

"You do know the way, right?" she asked. "This isn't some I'm-male-so-I-won't-ask-for-directions thing?"

He chuckled. "I know where I'm going. Promise."

"Have the Forgotten always lived here?"

"Define *here*."

Her brows came down to settle into a frown. "*Here* as in these mountains."

"Then no. We've moved quite a bit. The Dalshie are often in pursuit." Dominic pushed a branch aside for her, helped her over a log. The undergrowth was thickening, the waning sunlight even darker in this part of the forest. "But we tend to gravitate toward forests and open spaces. Nature helps us cope."

"With what?" she asked, but Dominic's answer was lost because at that moment they emerged from the trees into a huge clearing.

At least ten houses encircled the large grassy area. A fire pit was dug in the middle, surrounded by a ring of chairs. Each of the homes, more cottage than mansion, had porches that faced the center and lots of windows.

The space was dim—a lot darker than she might have expected, given that the sun hadn't quite set yet and it took Daughtry a minute to figure out why. The forest's canopy extended over the entire opening.

"The trees?" she asked, pointing up to the branches over-head. "They grew like that?"

"No, *we* grew them like that." Dominic chuckled at what was probably a shocked expression on her face. "What we can did is nothing. Haven't you ever seen a Rengalla work Earth magic?"

"No." She shook her head, causing him to frown slightly. "Have *you?*"

"Yes. When they came for us the first time."

She leaned in. "To Ravensbrück?"

A shudder seemed to wrack Dominic's body then he turned to her, eyes serious. "Be careful not to mention that name here. It's not something we wish to remember."

Bad memories—the way they entrapped a soul and stole future happiness was a concept that Daughtry was well familiar with. "I'm sorry," she said, frustration lacing her tone as she once again found herself without the necessary knowledge to navigate the situation. "I didn't know."

His lips quirked. "Hate that, do you?"

"More than you could know." She sighed. "Anything else I should avoid mentioning?"

"I'll give you the Cliff Notes." He swung a hand around the clearing. "Do you really not remember anything about this place?"

"Why would I remember? I've never been here before."

Her heart rate increased and a niggling began in the back of her mind. There *was* something familiar about the shaded clearing with its well-kept cottages. The wide expanse of green that was peacefully quiet.

"You spent almost a year here, Daughtry."

She shook her head mutely. "You're wrong."

Dominic turned, fixing her with those black eyes. "You really *don't* remember, do you?"

"There is *nothing* to remember," she said. Except, there was something in her subconscious, almost the imprint of a memory. "I-I—" A sigh. "No, I don't remember. Not exactly." Glancing around the space, she struggled to accept that her body seemed to remember this place, even if her mind didn't. She knew that the back door of the last cottage on the left was green, that there was a swing set less than a hundred feet into the forest straight ahead of them. She just didn't understand why she knew those things.

Her head tilted as she studied the path from which they had come, the trails littering the circle. She pointed at one to her right. "That one leads to a stream, right? One that's not too cold despite the mountain runoff?"

Dominic nodded. "Yes. It's a favorite spot for the children to swim."

Something about the way he said the last had her glancing up, trying to understand why the notion had brought pain to his words, his voice. "And the adults too?"

He smiled but it wasn't entirely joyful. "The adults too." A quick grin. "After the kids are in bed."

Her cheeks went a little hot. "Oh."

The silence between them stretched until Dominic broke it. "We used Earth magic to extend the branches, to fill in the leaves. Now we're shielded from prying eyes."

She took in the web of interwoven branches, understood that it must have taken immense skill to make it look both natural and beautiful. Rengalla could manipulate plants easily enough, but what was above her head could be considered art. "It's beautiful."

"I know," Dominic said. "I don't have their skill. My powers don't work like that."

Tell me about it, she wanted to say. *Try seeing death for a living.* "What can you do?"

"I'm a telepath." Her face froze and he laughed. "Don't worry. I can't read people's minds, I only hear if they project their thoughts to another person."

"You found her!"

The shout had her whirling around. Eric and Stephen ran up to them, glares on their faces.

"Whose idea was it?"

Daughtry hadn't heard that tone emerge from Dominic's mouth yet. The boys' faces transformed into mirrored guilty expressions and their shoulders slumped.

Even she stood up straighter.

But as she looked at the boys again, her mind caught what her eyes had missed before.

"Lift your sleeve," she ordered, stepping forward. Eric's face was confused but he complied.

Blue? She tried to wrap her mind around the markings, the way that a piercing indigo instead of black undulated up his forearms. The pattern was the same as the Dalshie's markings. It was just the color and the feelings radiating off those stains that were different.

If Dominic understood her surprise, his face didn't show it.

"Stephen?" she asked, her eyes widening at the brown clusters of lines scaling up his arms. "Do you have them anywhere else?" Her hand found the neck of his long-sleeved T-shirt, pulled it to the side as she tried to peer down it.

Stephen's face froze for a moment before a cocky smile spread across his face. "Anytime you want me to take off my shirt, all you have to do is ask, baby."

Oh yeah, she was *totally* into horny-as-hell teenagers.

She rolled her eyes. "Don't *baby* me. Where do they stop?"

"If you'd stop assaulting the under-aged boys, I'd show you."

She whirled to see an amused expression on Dominic's face. "Fine," she muttered and stepped back. "Just go and ruin all my fun."

His smile widened then he pulled off his shirt.

"Wow," she whispered, eyes glued to the skin he'd exposed.

"That's what they all say."

He was worse than the teenagers. "Shut up," she said, inching towards him. "You know I wasn't talking about your body." Not that it wasn't nice, but the markings were what had caught her gaze.

His hands came up in a gesture of surrender. "Shutting up."

Dominic was firmly muscled with broad shoulders, flat abs, and narrow hips. But those features hardly registered. What did was the fact that his markings crept up his arms, massing and climbing until they abruptly stopped at the tops of his shoulders.

If the blackness didn't represent something so intrinsically frightening, then she might have compared them to sleeves of tattoos.

But the staining wasn't as innocuous as a tattoo.

"Do they grow?"

He shook his head. "No further than this. Or not that we've seen. They appear at puberty and expand up the arms."

Questions filled her mind. "Can you do magic before they appear?"

"Sometimes."

"What—?" she started to ask but the arrival of three men cut her off.

"Grab her," the middle one ordered.

TWENTY

"WHAT THE HELL are you doing, Seth?" Dominic asked as he grabbed Daughtry's arm and pulled her parallel with him.

Seth, a barrel-chested man who was barely a few inches taller than Daughtry, scowled. "I know what *I'm* doing. I've been taking care of our people since you decided that you had to leave."

Some of the fight that had stiffened Dominic's form seemed to leech out of him with that statement. "I had to leave," he said. "You know it. But that still doesn't tell me what the fuck you're doing."

"We're going for the reward. Finder's fee is twenty percent."

Dominic's shoulders stiffened, and his voice hardened even further. "And you honestly think the Dalshie will pay?" He spat the words. "Are you fucking kidding? They'd rather kill you than blink at you twice."

Seth didn't back down. "Of course they'll pay. She's worth a ton."

"Lovely," Daughtry muttered the same time that Dominic murmured a series of insults under his breath. They seemed to involve quite a few creative derivatives of fucker, but even his extensive curse word vocabulary couldn't amuse her.

Because Seth meant to sell her to the Dalshie.

"They'll pay," Seth said as he closed the distance between them. Spittle formed at the corners of his mouth and his eyes, such a dark brown that they were almost black, were manic. "One way or another."

Dominic gave a harsh laugh. "You and what army, Seth? Our powers are pathetic when compared with theirs. It'd be a mission in death." His voice softened. "We ran from them because they wanted us to be slaves. They'll *never* pay. In fact, they'll probably kill us just for thinking they would."

Seth's expression went fierce as he clung to the stubborn hope. "They won't." A pause. "*This* will work. It's the only way . . ."

A crowd was gathering, talking amongst themselves uneasily as Seth continued to rant. But his words weren't convincing Dominic. And with each dismissed argument, Seth became further unhinged, until his voice was loud enough to echo through the clearing. Finally Dominic put up his hand. "I've heard enough. We don't work with the Dalshie. We won't turn Daughtry or any other innocent over to them."

"She's not innocent," Seth said, his eyes darkening in fury. "She's an Oracle. She's probably here to manipulate us and our futures!"

Daughtry's frustration had been building throughout the conversation but at that, she reached her breaking point. "I'm not here to hurt anyone! I'm here because those two morons brought me here—"

"Hey!" Eric said.

"It's true," she said then sighed. "Okay, maybe not the moron part, but the rest of it." Her voice steadied, quieting to a more reasonable volume. "I didn't even know that you were here. In fact, I was just leaving the area when these two grabbed me. I don't want any trouble, I just want to go."

"You can't—" Seth began.

"She can," Dominic said. "We have no reason to hold her here. If Daughtry wants to go she can do so." His eyes came up to hers. "I hope you'll at least stay the night. It gets darker than you can probably imagine out here once the sun sets. But if you don't want to, I'll get a flashlight and lead you out myself."

There was a tug on her sleeve and she glanced down. A little girl stood there, her two brown braids framing her nymph-like face.

"You're pretty," the girl said.

Daughtry felt her lips curl up into a smile when she would have thought it impossible just a few moments before. "Thanks."

Another tug brought her down and level with the little girl. "What's your name?" the girl asked.

"Daughtry. What's yours?"

"Laila." The girl's voice dropped to a whisper. "Guess what?"

"What?"

"My mom made cookies. Want to share some with me?"

Daughtry's heart expanded, fracturing the ice that had encased it the last couple of weeks, rebuilt supports she'd thought permanently broken.

"Are they oatmeal raisin?"

Laila wrinkled her nose. "No way."

"Then I'm in," Daughtry said with a chuckle. "But let me deal with the boys first, okay?"

Laila nodded.

When Daughtry stood, Seth and Dominic were still arguing, quieter but no less fierce.

"You may have been in charge while I was gone. But I'm

here now and we do not deal with those monsters." Dominic stepped forward until Seth had to tilt his head back in order to meet his eyes. "Yes, what the Dalshie did to us was awful, but we can't do *this*. Don't you understand? To turn Daughtry over would make us just like them."

"But—"

"The discussion is finished." Dominic looked up and addressed the crowd. "Go home, be with your families. Bring your concerns to me in the morning."

Seth wore an expression of such hatred that Daughtry's skin prickled. Then Dominic turned back to him and some of the fury faded.

"You're my friend, practically my brother," Dominic said. "I know that you're trying to do your best for us all. But this is not the way. It will never be the way."

"But—"

"No more for tonight."

Seth closed his mouth and turned away, shoulders stiff.

"I think you might have made an enemy," she said as Seth stalked to a house across the clearing.

"Seth is my friend, as good as blood for all the things we've endured together. We could never be enemies." Dominic flinched when the front door to the cottage slammed. "Family is and has always been the Forgotten's number one priority."

"That sounds nice." It was tacit agreement because Daughtry couldn't get past the hatred on Seth's face, the frost that had encased his eyes when he'd watched his brother.

Dominic might not be worried but she was.

All the better for her to be out of the encampment by first light.

"COME WITH US," Dominic told Eric and Stephen as he led Daughtry to his house. It sat on the opposite side of the clearing as Seth's but was larger and better kept.

A cross between a cottage and a craftsman, the house was cozy. Warm despite the slightly unused feeling it projected. He stooped to pull a key out of a planter and unlocked the door. Once they'd all crossed the threshold, he motioned for the kids to sit.

"Did they hurt you?" he asked Daughtry after she'd perched herself on an empty armchair.

She glanced around the room, an explosion of early nineties furnishings, complete with honey oak, sky blue, and lots—*lots*—of flowers, she started getting an uncomfortable feeling, very much like the class good girl being a tattletale.

"I'm fine," she said rather than actually answering the question.

Eric let out a small breath. It was a tiny sound of relief but she was glad that she'd been able to grant it. Despite his choice of companion in the wannabe-Lothario, Stephen, Eric seemed like a sweet kid.

"So you went with them willingly?" She felt the sharp bite of Dominic's disapproval at her non-answer.

"Um—"

"Yes or no?"

Her throat tightened when she looked at Eric, whose face was pale. Even Stephen appeared nervous, fingers fidgeting on his jeans. "No."

"Did they hurt you?"

She sighed, answered truthfully. "Only my head."

"Only your—" Dominic broke off, shook his own head. "You idiots!" he said, his face incredulous as he turned to the boys. "What the hell were you thinking?"

They coughed and squirmed on the plastic covered couch

cushions. Eric shoved Stephen hard, finally forcing the other boy to speak. The words didn't bring Daughtry any comfort.

"One of the girls sensed magic up the mountain. When we investigated, Seth recognized her. Said she wasn't to leave the mountain."

"*Seth* said!" Dominic sighed. "You listened to *him?* Eric, Stephen, you should know better."

Eric grumbled. "You're the one who left him in charge."

"No one else was willing!"

"I was," Stephen said.

"You're sixteen," Dominic said. "A fucking baby."

"I'm not a—"

"Real men don't abduct women!"

"Did you start the fire?" she asked, interrupting them.

Eric's eyes flew up. "How did you know?"

She shrugged, remembering the heat and speed with which the flames had moved. Though she hadn't noticed it while running for her life, now she could see that the timing was suspect.

"Fire?" Dominic asked. If he'd been in a cartoon, smoke would have been pouring out of his years. "*You* started the forest fire?"

Eric shook his head. "Seth did."

"Seth—" Dominic closed his eyes.

"Are you all related?" Daughtry asked, trying to steer the conversation into a different route. She and Dominic could talk more after the boys left.

The smallest flush appeared on Dominic's cheeks.

It was incongruous with the rest of him, the dark jeans, the fitted T-shirt. His olive skin and dark hair—even the single stud in his ear—made him more pirate than blushing schoolboy.

"Stephen and Eric are my cousins."

She clamped her mouth shut but was starting to feel like she was in some backwoods town where every hillbilly was related to everyone else.

"We're not all related," Dominic muttered, his eyes narrowed as if catching the drift of her thoughts despite her holding her tongue. "But many of us are. We came from the same camp, understand the same horrors, the same risks. That some have found love should be celebrated, not condemned."

A wave of cold washed over her, making Daughtry feel incredibly judgmental and ungrateful. He'd stood up for her and what had she done? Laughed at him?

"I'm sorry."

He was quiet for a moment. Then nodded and came over to her. "It's forgiven. But you should know that in this community, cousin is more often a way to honor closeness rather than actual genetic relationships."

He turned to the boys. "You can go. I'll see you both at dinner." His eyes narrowed. "We'll talk afterward."

Eric and Stephen had perked up at the word dinner, but when Dominic mentioned the talk, they both deflated. Still they nodded, dutifully standing then going out the door.

"Don't feel bad," Dominic said.

Her eyes flew up. "How do you know I feel bad?"

He gave a little smile. "You're an open book. Your emotions flow across your face like pictures across a television screen."

Cody had said that once. Sighing, she glanced to the ceiling as all the pain and failings from the past few weeks flowed through her. She should have known months ago that they wouldn't have worked.

A hand on her shoulder brought her to the present. "You okay?"

"Always," she assured him, though her confidence in that belief was fading as rapidly as the bond in her mind.

TWENTY-ONE

"YOU READY FOR THOSE COOKIES?"

Daughtry glanced up from the table where she'd been seated, trying futilely to drag Dominic's comb through her thick hair.

It was a war of attrition, with both her hair and the comb for the worse.

"Before dinner?" she quipped, struggling with a particularly bad strand.

"What's life if you can't have dessert first?"

"Okay—*ouch!* Dammit." Her scalp stung, and tears leaked from the corners of her eyes.

"Here let me help." Dominic picked up the comb and came towards her.

"No, that's okay. I—"

But he'd already grasped up a handful of her hair, and was working through it. "I used to do this for my sister."

She relaxed slightly when he didn't move to do anything further, just gently untangled the strands of her hair. Having a man so close to her was more intimate than she might have preferred, but the space Dominic kept between their bodies, the their respective memories fading. "Only eighty-six. And don't you know it's rude to ask a guy's age?"

Daughtry snorted. "Oh yeah, you sound so upset."

"I'm crying on the inside."

They sat in companionable silence for a while, Dominic combing her hair until she couldn't hold back the question that had been plaguing her. "Why did you leave?"

He sucked in a breath then released it slowly. Her hair blew across her neck, tickling the skin on her nape.

"I left to find the cure."

She jumped to her feet and whirled around so quickly that Dominic had to put his hands on her shoulders to steady her. "Cure for what?"

For the darkness? For the taint that transformed the Rengalla into soulless monsters?

The thought sent a surge of hope through her.

Because it would change *everything*.

His dark eyes were serious, his expression almost sad. "I'd hoped to find a way to change the Dalshie back."

"Do many Forgotten turn?" She was trying to understand why he cared. To protect his people? Or did they succumb to the darkness as well?

"No," he said. "None of us have ever transformed into a Dalshie."

"Then why?" she asked. Why search for something that would have no impact on his people?

"Eliminating the Dalshie would help everyone."

The unselfishness of that statement stunned her. He was so much like Cody, like the LexTals, that her heart throbbed. She missed him, missed the Colony, and the makeshift family she'd been building. But it wouldn't matter for long. Because the bond was so fragile that one more good shove would sever it forever.

robotic way with which he tackled the tangles made it almost impersonal.

"Does your sister brush her own hair now?"

"No." The harshness of that word made her stiffen and turn her head to take in the bleakness of his expression. "No," he said again, though quieter. "She's dead."

"I'm sorry." There was hesitation on her side as she wondered how to carry on the conversation.

"Just ask."

"What?" She rotated fully, knocking the comb from his hand to the floor. The plastic hitting the tile made a louder noise than she would have expected.

"How she died," he said, his voice having gone almost flat. "Or don't. You don't have to, it was my fault."

"I'm sure it wasn't—"

With a curse, he turned away. "I chose the route we traveled home. I was careless. I got us caught and brought to that camp."

The air in her lungs froze and a long moment passed before her brain kicked in and her breathing commenced. "What happened?" she asked. It was a soft question, instinct telling her that harshness might shatter Dominic's hard exterior.

"I was tired. We'd been shopping, gathering supplies for our family to flee Germany. I thought we could take a shortcut." He swallowed hard. "I was wrong." He shook his head like he was trying to shake off the stranglehold of old memories. "When I told her to run, she did. They shot her in the back."

There was something warm and wet running down Daughtry's cheeks. She brushed her hands across her face, was surprised to find that she was crying. "Did she . . . ?" Had his sister's misery ended then?

"No." He sucked in a breath. "Not then. Katalina suffered for days, crammed body to body on the train before she succumbed."

Daughtry's touch on his arm was tentative, a gentle comfort. "I'm so sorry you both had to endure that."

"Me too." Dominic's voice went a little firmer. "The only thing I'm grateful for is that she didn't have to endure the experiments."

"That bad?"

"Worse." He scooped up the comb from the floor and gestured for her to turn around. She obliged, knowing that sometimes the truth was easier to divulge without eye contact. "Injections, electrocutions, gas, burnings. If they could imagine it, they did it." His fingers shook as he brushed her hair. "The worst was their gleaming red eyes through the observation windows. The way they took joy in doing harm."

Her own memories of her time with the Dalshie flooded over her. She'd had a vision of herself strapped helplessly before them, at the mercy of their cruelty and their weapons, but had managed to avert it.

Would Dominic's fate have been her own, if she'd failed?

Had Caroline's torture been just as bad?

Undoubtedly, she thought, feeling sympathy for Cody's sister all over again.

"It was the magical experiments that were the worst."

"What did they do?"

His hands halted on her scalp and a jagged chuckle emerged from his throat. "Did you know that I never believed in magic? Not until they strapped me down and filled my body with it."

She sucked in a breath.

"Most of my group died," Dominic said. "The few of us that survived were grouped together and filled with more power, more darkness. Until finally some of us were able to do magic on our own."

"Did you—?" She wasn't sure what she wanted to ask. Why

had he survived when the others hadn't? But it seemed t a question.

The comb began to move again. "We think the rea lived was because of our DNA. Every one of us can tr lineage back to a small principality in what is today l Europe."

"What's so special about that place?"

There was a long pause. "I'm not sure. All I *do* know the Forgotten are from different countries, different ethn and, have varied upbringings. There are no similarities— aside from the related ancestry."

"I'm so sorry Dominic."

His hands moved as he gave what she assumed was a sh "The past is the past. The only thing we can do now is to n forward."

"I'm still—"

"I remember seeing the group of Rengalla come to camp," Dominic said. "Thinking that the rainbow of glow strands of magic would save us." A shake of his head. "Then Dalshie teleported us away. It wasn't until years later that were strong or organized enough to escape."

"Do they still pursue you?"

His fingers tensed then relaxed. "For awhile they relentless and we spent more time fleeing than living. Now seem to have found another target. We've been in this spc almost twenty years."

"And you age like them? Like *us*?"

"I guess. We stop showing signs of aging in our mid-ties." She felt him shrug. "There are worse ages to s suppose. At least I don't get carded."

"So you're what? Ninety?"

He chuckled at her question, the tension of the mom

As a human, the troubles of the Forgotten, of the Dalshie, and Rengalla would no longer affect her.

"Oh." A sharp pain jabbed her gut at the thought.

She didn't need a cure. The bond would break and she'd lose her powers anyway. So there was no reason for her stomach to be churning, her throat burning.

No reason except for the little voice inside of her that kept screaming for her to keep her hopes up. Instead of the devil on her shoulder, she had the eternal optimist.

It was no less damaging.

Because dashed dreams could be just as deadly as immoral acts.

"Hey. I—"

"Take your hands off of her."

Her mouth dropped open and her knees wobbled. She almost dropped straight onto the floor. Because he couldn't be here.

He. Could. Not. Be. Here.

Not when he'd ripped her heart out and lit it on fire. Not when he'd—for all intents and purposes—chucked the burning embers off a freaking cliff.

No. Her mind was playing tricks on her.

Because that niggling, the slightest pressure that had been bearing down on her mind for the last hours it *couldn't* be because of him.

Dominic removed his hands but instead of stepping back, he placed himself between her and their intruder. Emerald eyes were filled with fury, and the small place in her mind devoted to the man opposite her boiled with anger.

Cody took two steps forward, and shoved Dominic out of the way.

He grabbed her. Yanked her against his chest.

His lips slammed down onto hers.

TWENTY-TWO

SHE WRENCHED HER HEAD AWAY, shoving against Cody with every bit of strength she possessed.

Why would he touch her, *kiss* her after everything that had been said and done? How could he just walk up to her and take what he wanted without considering how it would tear her to shreds?

The slap of her palm across his cheek was loud.

Silence descended. Thick. Stifling. She stared at the growing red mark on his face, horrified at her behavior. At his.

Regret—no, *disgust*—overtook her and she turned away.

Cody was there, hands on her shoulders, forcing her to face him. His arms were strong bands that pinned hers to her sides. That the contact could feel so right even when it was so wrong alarmed her, enraged her, *shattered* her.

She beat at his chest. "Let me go!" Her struggling was pointless. She'd always loved how strong Cody was, how he made her feel so safe.

His strength was turning out to be her worst enemy.

"You heard her."

Dominic's cool voice flowed over her, settling some of her

nerves. He'd prevented Seth from selling her to the Dalshie, surely his kindness would extend to this.

Her eyes flew over Cody's shoulder, taking in the frown lines embedded around Dominic's mouth. Daughtry didn't want to draw him into her conflict but she was in agony. Cody's embrace brought only pain.

"Please," she whispered.

Dominic stepped forward, almost bumping into Cody. "Release her."

"Fuck off."

"I'm rubber and you're glue."

Cody's stare finally withdrew from Daughtry, rotated to unleash a fierce scowl on Dominic. "What the fuck are you talking about?"

Daughtry had no clue, but Cody's grip had loosened. She slipped back, rounding the dining room table to keep it between them. His gaze found her, traced her body, which was clad only in a loose pair of sweats and a baggy T-shirt, hungrily.

"Works every time," Dominic said, his lips turned up though his dark eyes were serious.

There was no warning.

Within a second, Cody had turned and was knocking Dominic to the ground.

They rolled, fists connecting with *thunks*, legs sprawling and knocking chairs to the wayside.

The curses burned her ears.

Cody's head whipped back, blood pouring out his nose when Dominic's elbow connected. Her heart galloped, threatened to burst from her chest. She was always surprised how quickly violence could erupt.

How long it took her to react disappointed her.

Her body revolted against the idea of either man hurt. Cody was sewn into the fabric of her heart, her soul. Dominic—almost a complete stranger—had shown more kindness to her than almost every other person in her life. He was suddenly pushed backwards, sliding across the tile floor to slam into a bank of cabinets.

Cody stood to follow him but Daughtry was faster.

She shoved herself between the two men, standing guard over Dominic, preventing Cody from taking another shot.

"I do have some honor, cowgirl," he said. "I don't hit a man when he's down."

The words were out of her mouth before she even processed them. "No, you only do that with women."

Emotions clouded Cody's face, regret, disappointment—and the one she was trying to pretend didn't exist—*pain*.

He couldn't be hurt, not when he'd so effectively pushed her away, not when he'd cut her down to the very fabric of her soul.

"I—"

His words were interrupted by Dominic's groan. He stumbled to his feet, holding his side. "You could have warned me about that right hook."

Daughtry grimaced, guilt over drawing him into her fight inundating her. "I'm sorry—"

"Why are you still here?" Cody interrupted.

He didn't try to touch her again, just came close, the heat from his chest warming her back.

"Because, despite your *honor*"—Dominic practically spat the word—"I don't condone the manhandling of women."

"She's mine."

Dominic's brows rose, eyes passing between her and Cody. "I'd ask her opinion on that, dude."

Cody's anger rose, almost scalding her across the bond with its intensity.

She was abruptly exhausted—and too tired to deal with

another fight between the men. She glanced over at Dominic. "Could you give us a minute?"

"You sure?" His concern was evident, touching even, but not necessary because she'd cope with whatever storm Cody was bringing.

"She's sure," the emerald-eyed warrior at her back snapped.

With a sigh, she nodded. "*I'm* sure."

When Dominic left, Daughtry stepped to the side, not wanting to give Cody the chance to corner her. His every touch was rending—the feelings of rightness at the contact warring with the pain of his betrayal, his harsh words, his abandonment.

As she was bending to right one of the chairs, Cody spoke. "Sweetheart—"

"Wrong word to start off with," she said. "You've made it very clear what I am to you."

"It's not like that." Cody sighed and grabbed another chair then shoved it towards the table. "Just sit. Please," he added when she bristled.

Her steps were hesitant but she took the seat he offered. Cody crouched in front of her, keeping eye contact. When he would have rested his hands on her thighs, she leaned back and shook her head.

Wasn't happening.

He didn't speak for a long moment and when he finally did, the words didn't heal the gaping wound in her heart. "I was pissed," he said. "So damned pissed when Caroline came back."

She snorted. That wasn't exactly news.

"I wasn't mad at you, not at all." He paused. "But then I was. It was *your* fault that she'd been captured, your fault that you have the powers that you do. It was your fault that you're so goddamned valuable to the Dalshie."

Flinching, she started to push the chair back. Each statement was a hot splinter under her fingernail, a dagger to the gut.

She couldn't breathe. Her eyes burned, and frost sank into her limbs, her heart.

Cody grabbed the chair to keep it in place. "No. I don't mean it like that. Logically, I knew it wasn't your fault." His gaze dropped for a second before it flew back up to hers. "I *know* it's not your fault. It's just that I had . . . all of these *feelings*. They didn't make sense, but they filled me, overwhelmed my thoughts until I couldn't remember *not* blaming you, until the single thing I could focus on was you and how Caroline getting hurt was all your fault."

Pushing his arm out of the way, she stood. "Those are called emotions, Cody. Normal people have them all of the time."

"They *weren't* normal!" Cody started to reach for her, then stopped and dropped his arms to his sides. "They weren't *my* feelings. I don't know how else to explain it. These thoughts would invade my mind." His eyes dropped to the floor, an action so unlike him that Daughtry managed to quiet the maelstrom in her mind and focus on his words.

"They were almost normal," he said. "*Almost* right. Except, and it took me a long time to realize this, but there was always something a little off about them." He cleared his throat, discomfort marring his features. "It's just . . . there would be so many of them that I'd forget that anything was wrong. It made it seem like I had always had them."

She frowned. "I don't understand."

Wasn't sure if she wanted to. Not if it brought her more pain.

"The longer I was away from the Colony, the less thoughts I had. When I came after you while you were working on Kaitlin's vision, I started to feel normal. I wanted to protect you." His voice dropped. "To be with you. To *love* you. Then I saw you with Morgan, saw him touch you, and I couldn't remember any of the reasons I'd come in the first place."

She wondered what would have happened if Cody been able to hold on to his reasons, if he'd somehow managed to say something, and whether it would have made one bit of difference. He'd jumped to conclusions about Morgan, which had pissed her off. Would she have been willing to listen to anything he might have said?

She would have, she decided after a moment. At that point only a few of the links between them had been cut. Her heart and mind had still been so desperate for the connection.

Nothing like the cool numbness that filled her as their separation progressed.

"Because I saw you with Morgan." A pause. "What I said was awful. You were right to tell me to leave."

"That's why you gave me the flowers."

He nodded. "I scheduled the delivery as soon I got back. But by the time they arrived, Caroline needed to get away from the Colony. The prying eyes, the pitying stares are too much for her."

Daughtry didn't like the prickling Cody's words raised on her nape. "You mean I'm too much for her."

There was a beat of silence before he shrugged. "Can you really blame her? You look like—" His mouth snapped closed. "I'm sorry."

"Don't be." She turned away from the conversation, straightened a few items on the counter, snatched up a dishrag to wipe the tiles. Maybe her movements would make her forget that her heart was bruised, perhaps damaged beyond repair.

"Daughtry."

The hand on her shoulder made her stiffen.

"Dammit," Cody said, quietly but no less intense. "I can't even touch you now? After everything we've been through?"

She thought of all of the betrayals, the cruel words, the pushing her away over and over. She couldn't completely discount that there had been good times, that they'd shared an intimacy that had filled her to her very core. But because he was so close to her heart, interwoven into her very soul, his ability to wound her was greater than anyone else's.

"I'm sorry, Cody," she said.

Her teeth clamped down on her tongue in an effort to hold back the sobs that were squeezing her chest, choking her. She wished for the numbness that had filled her before, found she was unable to grasp it.

"No," she said when she could speak again. "I don't think you have the right to touch me. Not any longer."

"But—"

She swallowed roughly. "No. No more."

Then she bolted for the back door.

TWENTY-THREE

HER VISION WAS BLURRY, her footsteps rapid as she headed for the isolation of the trees.

A tug on her hand made her gasp.

"I thought you were going to have cookies with us."

It was Laila. The sweet precociousness of the little girl was so far from how Daughtry felt at the moment that she wanted to yank her hand back and sprint away. But she wouldn't hurt someone else. Not just because her mind and her heart were fractured.

"Why are you crying?" Laila asked into the silence. "Are you sad?"

Some of the franticness that buzzed through her limbs faded. Her mind cleared and her pulse slowed. She could focus again, was surprised to find that her lips had curved up slightly.

Laila's explanation was a simple one. Yet so right.

"Yes," she told the little girl. "I'm sad."

"My mom always says that cookies make you happy." Laila's face screwed up. "Well, she says that chocolate makes girls happy and there's chocolate in the cookies, so that has to work, right?"

Daughtry laughed softly, amusement soaking into her like the final rays of the muted sunshine flowing through the canopy overhead. "You're determined, aren't you?" She couldn't fault the girl's logic either. Chocolate was the perfect cure for a broken heart.

Laila shrugged, unrepentant, her brown braids bobbing around her head. "Mom says that I can only have a cookie before dinner if I share them with you." A pause that spoke of more intuition than Daughtry would have expected from someone so young. "And I don't like it when people are sad."

Her heart squeezed, the soft words rubbing right against its vulnerable underbelly. "Alright then," she said. "Let's do it."

Despite whatever else was going on in her life, obliging Laila was easy—a simple solution to a simple problem when Daughtry seemed to only be surrounded by complications.

She followed Laila down the path from Dominic's cottage and past three smaller homes. They clomped up the wooden steps of the fourth, a pale green home with white trim and shutters. Window boxes were filled with marigolds and roses, and trimmed bushes framed the stairs. A delicious smell radiating from the open windows made a wave of homecoming wash over Daughtry, coating her so completely from hair to soles that she felt the last lingering pain from her encounter with Cody slide into the recesses of her mind.

The memories, the agony of her situation would no doubt return later. But for now she was able to concentrate on the present.

Namely getting that little girl her cookie.

"Come on!" She was startled to see the screen door had been opened and Laila was waving her impatiently forward. "They're done!"

She followed Laila directly into the kitchen, a small and cozy space with dark cabinets and pale countertops.

Laila was right. The cookies were done, plated and sitting on top of a scarred table that filled most of the open floor.

"Mommy! I brought her!"

A slim figure walked into the room and Daughtry felt a shiver run down her spine. She knew the woman, was almost sure of it.

That thought was confirmed when Laila's mother swooped across the room and wrapped Daughtry in an embrace.

"I'm so happy you're back. So happy you're safe."

There was such familiarity in being in the other woman's arms that Daughtry didn't pull away. Touch still wasn't an entirely comfortable concept for her to cope with, but between the bond's shield and the casual contact she'd gotten used to at the Colony, at least she didn't freak out.

"Do I know you?" Her question was soft, hesitant. She didn't want to hurt the other woman. Not when her soul told her that the woman was important.

"Do you—" The other woman's statement was halted as she leaned back and regarded Daughtry with a clear blue gaze. "It's me. Brigette. Surely you haven't forgotten me?"

Daughtry pulled free. "I'm sorry. I've forgotten lots of things." She shook her head in frustration. "My mind was filled with blocks. They've affected my memories."

"Oh."

There was such disappointment in that single syllable that Daughtry found herself apologizing. "I'm sorry. I didn't mean to forget. I just—"

Brigette put her hand up, her eyes on Laila who was watching the conversation with wide eyes. "Get two plates please. You can each have two cookies."

Daughtry's mouth was so dry that she wasn't sure she could choke anything down, chocolate or not. But when she began to refuse the sweets, Brigette turned away and left the room.

"Here you go!"

Laila shoved a plate in her hand, her mouth already full of cookie.

Daughtry looked down at the dish, a sky blue circle with a border of white hearts. Her stomach lurched. Because there was something in her mind, a niggling in the mess of thoughts buried deep. But what was it?

She strained, reached for it—

Something slammed down on the table behind her, startling her, loosening her fingers so that the plate slipped from her grasp.

It hit the floor and shattered.

A memory slammed into her—

Voices argued. A deep masculine tone competing with a higher pitched feminine one. The kitchen was almost the same, except the cabinets were lighter, the furniture older.

Daniel, her adopted father, stood with his back against the doorframe. Judith, her pseudo-mother, gripped the sink.

"I'm not leaving."

The terse words were Judith's.

"We must." Daniel crossed the room. "We can't lead the Dalshie here. Not after all the Forgotten have done for us. It was fine for a short time, but the Dalshie are closing in. One of the women even sensed their magic nearby."

"The Dalshie have already left! There's no risk to this place." *Judith slammed her hands on the counter. "And we're Forgotten too! We deserve peace after all of the trouble the brat has brought us."*

"The Dalshie ordered us to keep her near San Diego. We moved without their permission, they'll—"

"Why can't we just let her find her own way? Dump in her an orphanage, throw her from a damn cliff, I don't care."

"The Dalshie know this settlement is here. They've only left

it alone because the Forgotten haven't crossed them, because they have other things they think are more important."

Daniel touched his wife's arm, but she shrugged him off. "They want Daughtry. You know they'll come here for her unless we do as they say. We can't risk the others." A pause. "We can't risk Thomas."

"I don't want to leave him!" It was a wail, accompanied by tears and a collapse to the ground.

Daughtry had seen it often enough to know what would happen. Daniel would wrap Judith in his arms, would capitulate with any request.

She shrank back into the shadows and almost shrieked when she bumped into someone.

"Daughtry, it's just me."

Thomas. Her friend. Her adopted brother. More family than the two people in the other room—

Past morphed with the present as Daughtry saw her fourteen-year old self interact with a tall, lanky Thomas. His blond hair was the same style as it had been when she'd last seen him, but in the memory, he was thinner—not the adult she'd seen murdered.

His body was whole, his skin intact. He was nothing like the tortured, shredded being she'd seen in the dungeon of the Dalshie's compound.

The memory of her time in captivity threatened to overtake this one. But she managed to hold on to the thread of her past, mostly because she needed a picture of Thomas in her mind that wasn't laced with cruelty and pain, with torture and screams.

"You don't have to go," he said, his voice barely a whisper. He didn't want his parents to know they were eavesdropping.

Her younger self's shoulders slumped. "Yes. I think I do."

"Daughtry." She stopped, but didn't turn around. "They love

you," he said then winced. "In their own way."

"Yeah." It was easier to agree than to argue the truth.

Then she walked up the stairs, packed up her suitcase, and climbed out her window.

It hadn't been soon enough, she realized, images flying through her brain. Because before she'd fully hit the forest, the Dalshie had arrived.

They'd taken Thomas.

Altered her memories.

Daughtry remembered thinking that she'd been staring into a mirror, as bright violet eyes had locked onto hers and poured magic into her brain.

Her next memory was starting a new school in Northern California—

Blinking, she found herself ten years in the future, back in a similar kitchen. Her legs shook and she fumbled her way over to a chair then sank down into it.

Same encampment, different time. Same despair, different reason for her shredded heart.

A small hand clasped with hers. "You're not alone."

Tears filled her eyes. "I'm sorry," she told Laila, to Brigette. "I'm a wreck."

Brigette's gaze met hers. "Don't be sorry. You've been through a lot. Here." She pushed a book across the table towards her.

Daughtry opened the cover, was surprised to recognize her own handwriting. Hand-drawn doodles filled the margins, cut out pictures from magazines were plastered across the pages, just like the diary she'd found at the house in California.

Except this one had something else that one hadn't—

Dream Journal was written in familiar scrawl in a section marked off with a scrap of ribbon. Beneath the heading were a series of dates, detailed descriptions, and even more drawings.

She gasped as she realized what they were. Memories. Or fragments of them. From her time with her biological parents—before Judith and Daniel—from her initial years at the Colony.

JUNE 7TH

Today I remembered blowing out candles on a birthday cake. The two adults surrounding me weren't Judith and Daniel. They were different. And they looked at me like they loved me. There were five candles on the cake and a pile of presents with princess wrapping paper on the table next to me—

"IT WAS YOUR IDEA," Daughtry gasped, the memories flowing through her. She'd spent a lot of time in this kitchen, had shared her fears, her pain, her strange dreams. It had been Brigette's idea to keep a journal of them. "You knew something."

She remembered now. How she'd often escaped the tension at her house by coming to Brigette's. The other woman had welcomed Daughtry with open arms, listening to her complain about Judith and Daniel on a regular basis, advising her to write down the strange dreams that seemed to plague her. She'd been kind and more of a mother figure than Judith had ever been.

They'd made cookies, watched movies. Brigette had been . . . family.

"You remember?"

Daughtry closed her eyes then opened them. "You never would give me the recipe to your double chocolate chunk cookies."

"I'd have to kill you if I did." Brigette's eyes twinkled for a moment before sobering. "Are you okay?"

Dee sighed. "Honestly? I hardly know. Everything is so jumbled up." She held up the journal. "How?"

How had Brigette known the dreams were more?

"I suspected," she said. "When you told me about your dreams, I thought they were too detailed, too complete. I hoped they might be something *more*."

Daughtry nodded.

"I have a different ability than most of the Forgotten," Brigette said. "I can sense people's pain, sometimes even remove it." Her expression softened. "And you're filled to the brim with it now. Why? What's happened?"

"It's—" Daughtry shook her head, not willing to reopen the wounds that were tentatively scabbed over. "Does Laila have the same ability?"

"Yes." Brigette shared a long look with her daughter. "But she's not supposed to use her abilities. Sometimes she doesn't understand all of the complications that come with manipulating someone's emotions."

Having seen firsthand the implications of such manipulations herself—her blocked mind and memories still piecemeal at best—Daughtry knew the consequences could be much more far-reaching than first thought. And despite the gravity of their abilities, she still felt a little jealous. Laila and Brigette could heal with their minds, remove a person's suffering.

That in itself was more noble than an ability to alter death.

She wondered if any of the Rengalla could heal with their minds. Cody, Tyler, and Suz could all reknit skin, fix bones and sometimes even organs. But could they heal depression? Or another mental illness?

A knock at the door drew all of their attention. Dominic entered, a bruise marring the skin above his cheekbone. His face was placid, though his eyes were concerned.

"Got any more of those cookies?" he asked, plunking himself into the chair opposite Daughtry. He glanced at Brigette. "Did you show her the journal yet?"

TWENTY-FOUR

DINNER WAS A ROWDY AFFAIR. Long tables had been set up in the clearing and the fire pit was lit. Hamburgers and hot dogs were passed around on paper plates. Corn on the cobs, still in their husks, sat in baskets on the picnic tables, along with potato salad, fruit, and more plates of Brigette's delicious cookies.

Daughtry listened more than she spoke, enjoying the conversations flowing around her. Despite getting more than her fair share of curious looks, being seated between Laila and Dominic and across from Brigette afforded her a certain amount of question-free space.

The Forgotten's eyes weren't the only ones on her, however.

A pair of green irises, framed by a handsome face she knew as well as her own, had been locked onto her for the entirety of the meal. He sat at the end of the row of tables, his own question-free space gained not by the barrier of others but by the frustration and anger radiating off him.

Cody was impossible to ignore and not just because of his physical presence.

His mind was a pulsing beacon across the bond. The link

that had been withered just hours before was no longer weak-ening, wasn't at risk of snapping. Instead, it was thicker, stronger.

Because he was there.

The connection felt tender, almost raw, and she wanted to scream at him to leave her alone. He wouldn't stick around, eventually he would put her at a distance and and she couldn't take the push-pull. And so a part of her even wished for the bond to break already, to put her out of her misery. But with Cody there, that wasn't going to happen.

A deeper part of her, the piece she was trying to ignore was glad their connection remained.

And that scared her more than anything. Because what kind of person would take back a man who treated her like Cody had?

Except there was what he'd been trying to tell her—the explanation that threatened to undermine every barrier she'd so carefully erected around her heart the last couple of days. She should hear him out, probably even owed him the time to explain. But . . .

She was scared.

What if the reason he'd pushed her away wasn't good enough?

What if *she* wasn't good enough?

He'd leave again and—

"You look awfully thoughtful," Dominic said. He leaned close to talk over the din of the crowd.

A wave of disapproval slid down the bond.

"I've got a lot on my mind," she said, ignoring the link, the way his possessiveness made a small part of her preen in approval.

She was sick. Literally screwed in the head. Going in circles that kept leading her back to the same exact place.

Cody. Their connection. The fact that he was sewn deeply into her soul.

Maybe Brigette could cure her.

"He seems pleasant," he said with a nod to Cody.

Her bondmate had stood, was staring at her with his arms crossed, his back against a tree. He hadn't eaten, and might as well have been a statue for as still as he was.

"It's complicated," she told Dominic.

"So *un*-complicate it," Brigette said, interjecting into the conversation. Laila had run off and she slid into the empty chair next to Daughtry.

"I—" She shook her head, knowing the story of the roller coaster that had led her into a relationship with Cody was too long and twisted to relay over dinner. He had a lot of good qualities, was extremely loyal to his inner circle.

Just not her.

For whatever reason, Daughtry had never made it that far.

"That's bullshit." Cody's voice snapped across the bond. *"You're the most important person in my life."*

She couldn't hold back her snort. *"Then I don't want to be. Because if this is how you treat the person who supposedly means the world—"*

Dominic coughed but when she glanced up at him, his eyes were on his plate.

Brigette was staring at her with a perplexed expression on her face.

"Sorry," Daughtry said, then bit her lip, wondering if she could explain and how much. Because, while Brigette exuded comfort and familiarity, she wasn't exactly a lay-her-heart-on-the-line kind of girl.

After a moment, she said, "You remember what Daniel and Judith were like." Brigette nodded. "The guy before Cody was exactly like them." Controlling, verbally abusive, self-esteem stomping. "Then there was Cody. It was a struggle, since we both fought against the relationship. But by the time we agreed to take the chance, I thought he was different."

"And?" It was a soft question but not from Dominic or Brigette. Daughtry whirled, and met Cody's stare. How he'd approached without her sensing was a testament to his military training. Once she'd met his eyes, he asked, "You don't think I'm different from Jimmy?"

He waited for her answer, their minds linked, their bodies within reach, and yet they might as well have been miles apart.

"I don't know *what* to think."

She sighed, pushed to her feet, and after waving off Dominic when he would have followed her, left the table. When Cody trailed her, she didn't protest. "I'm tired of the roller coaster, I'm tired of being pulled in and then burned. I'm tired of not being lo—" She clamped her lips tight, biting hard on her bottom one, willing the freaking tears to be held at bay just one more time. Because she couldn't be weak. Not again. Not when Cody had seen her that way too many times already.

"I don't think you're weak. I think you're perfect." He clutched her arm with his hand, his fingers warm, his grip almost painfully tight. "Dammit, cowgirl! Look at me. *See* me."

"I can't!" She wrenched free and sprinted for the forest. Her stomach churned, the tears she'd tried to hold back poured forth.

"Stop."

"Stop!"

"No," she murmured, not sure if she was answering the mental command or merely attempting to deny his renewed intimacy.

Because his mind linked with hers felt right.

Her magic called to his and vice versa. The urge to connect was interwoven with her DNA, her every cell. Just his voice in her mind made her want to forget the past.

Daughtry stumbled.

One second she was running, glancing back over her shoulder, watching as Cody closed the gap between them. The next she was skidding across the forest floor. It took a long moment for her lungs to inflate properly and then she curled in on herself, huddling into a ball as tears burned tracks down her cheeks. Her sobs were wrenching, hurting her throat, her lungs.

Her heart.

But Cody was there. He wrapped his arms around her, and pulled her into his lap.

"Shh. It's okay."

That only made her cry harder. Because *nothing* was okay. How could anything ever be all right ever again?

She couldn't catch her breath, her lungs burned from the exertion of her tears.

"Good God, cowgirl. Please stop. I'm sorry. I'm so sorry."

He turned her, pressed her tightly against his chest, his vice-like grip the only thing that managed to slow her breathing.

The tears stopped long before the sobs.

Finally—*finally*—her pulse slowed, her inhalations leveled out, and she pushed back from Cody.

There was a pulse of pain along the bond before he let her go.

But it wasn't like she could go far. Exhaustion made her chest hurt, her movements weak and clumsy. And when she tried to stand, her head spun.

He caught her before she fell for a second time.

"I've got you," he said as he swept her into his arms.

That was what she was afraid of.

It took a few minutes for her to realize that he was carrying her deeper into the forest. "What are you doing?"

"We need to talk."

Anger coursed through her. "So what? You're just going to kidnap me?"

"Seemed like the best idea at the time." He glanced at her, one corner of his mouth curving just the slightest bit. The bond was inconsistent, her ability to read his thoughts coming in and out. But she didn't need a mental link to recognize that expression.

"Put the smirk away," she said. "It won't work on me."

The other half of his mouth went up.

"Am I so amusing?" she asked, her throbbing lungs ramping her anger, the sadness of the previous moment vanishing like so much smoke. If Cody wanted her to take him on, then she'd do it.

She'd succeed, too. In his arms or not.

"I'll take pissed over the silent treatment any day." He readjusted his grip on her when she squirmed, attempting to extract herself, and stepped over a log, navigating the dark forest like the capable soldier he was. Sure-footed and unwavering.

"I wish that were the case," he said softly.

All of his thoughts may not be reaching her mind, but his emotions were billboard loud.

The main one was regret.

But without the evidence of his thoughts, how was she to know whether his regret was because he'd hurt her or because he'd risked losing his powers?

"Why can you hear me more?" It had been that way in the past, when the manipulations, the blocks had still existed in her mind.

His smirk faded. "Because I've let you in. You've barricaded yourself against me."

"Can you blame me?" She pointed to a rock before he could answer. "Can you put me down over there? My back is hurting."

He deposited her on the boulder and squatted in front of

her. Before she could tell him she was fine, green sparks shot from his palms and fluttered to her chest, soaking into her skin.

The heat of his magic was intense but faded almost immediately, taking the pain with it.

"You've got your powers back."

"It would seem so." He didn't glance up at her, just rose and brushed his hands on his jean. He didn't say was what they both knew. That he'd come back for that very reason.

"No." Such vehemence in those two letters. Her eyes flew up.

"So why? Why'd you come for me?" she asked. "You wanted to be rid of me so desperately. Why pursue me after I'd left?" She shook her head. "The only logical reason I can come up with is that you didn't want to lose your magic."

"No," he said again. "I lived ninety-odd years without functioning powers. I could survive more without them."

"Then why?" she asked, frustration filled her. Each of her questions was punctuated by a push against his chest. "Why didn't you leave me? Did you take pleasure in breaking my heart? Once wasn't enough? You want to do it again?"

Instead of stepping away as she'd hoped, Cody came closer. "I felt your fear."

"Wh-what?"

"You were terrified. It punched through into my mind as effortlessly as lightning. I had already started feeling a little different after spending those few days at the cabin—almost like myself again—and when Morgan teleported back to the Colony telling me you were gone, I tried to make him take me back to the cabin." He banged his fist on his thigh.

"He wouldn't." Cody shoved a hand through his hair. "He wanted to talk to Dante, to come up with a plan to expand on the search he'd already conducted of the area around the cabin. But when I felt that bolt of fear I made him take me back." He swallowed. "I tracked you and with every mile I closed between us, the fog of thoughts around my mind, around the bond faded. I saw how withered it looked, how it was almost broken."

He shook his head, helped her down from the rock. "Pushing you away had seemed natural, the right thing to do. But the further I was from the Colony, the more everything became clear." He sighed. "I should have tried harder after I saved you from the fire, but I didn't really know how to explain. More than that, I didn't understand what I was feeling."

"I didn't give you the chance," she murmured. Not at that point. She'd been too hurt, too closed off to listen.

He squeezed her hand. "I should have tried harder anyway."

As they walked, she considered what Cody had told her. He must have felt her when she thought Dominic was a Dalshie. Daughtry couldn't think of any time over the last day when she'd felt more fear. It had swarmed her every nerve, activated her flight response.

But that would mean that those feelings had needed to travel a distance that was greater than anything the bond had ever managed before.

Did that mean their connection was more ingrained than she'd imagined? Would she ever really be free of it? Especially if the feelings for the man standing next to her refused to go away.

There was also the fact she was trying to ignore, the piece she was gripping tightly because it kept her safe.

If Cody really cared so little about her, why had he come?

She closed her eyes. "What became clear?"

"What?"

"As you got further from the Colony, what exactly got clearer?"

It didn't make sense. He'd left several times over the course of Caroline returning. Never once had the old Cody made an appearance as a result.

Except . . . the jealousy with Morgan. The violet—

"That I love you."

She shook her head. That couldn't be true, not after everything.

"Feel it, cowgirl," he said. "I can't live a day without you, let alone a lifetime." He laced his fingers with hers, brought them to his chest. "My heart is yours. Without you in my life, the beats are just pulses of blood. Your presence, your *existence* turns that liquid into emotions, into memories."

Her fingers spasmed, fighting against the soft rhythm of the organ locked beneath his rib cage. She didn't want to hear him, to sense the honesty barreling down the bond and enveloping her.

"Please," Cody said. "You're it for me. My chance for love, my hope for the future. Without you nothing matters."

The words were one thing. But the emotions pouring across the bond, rejuvenating the crumbling ropes of their intermixed powers, thickening it, bringing it back to life . . . those were so much more.

It was impossible to resist.

Yet she must.

Because if she didn't, the next time she might find herself irrevocably broken.

"Don't," Cody said, stroking a finger down her cheek. "Don't shut me out. Hear me. Use the bond. Feel what I'm feeling."

She leaned back, still trapped in his embrace. "That doesn't matter!"

"The hell is doesn't."

"You'll just push me away again," she said. "It might be a week from now, a year, a decade. And I can't take it again."

Cody released her, then turned away and cursed. "Haven't you heard anything I've said? It's like my thoughts were surrounded in a fog." He stopped. "I couldn't think straight, my emotions weren't consistent. They didn't even feel like mine. It was like the Colony was somehow poisoning my thoughts, making me think the worst of you, when deep down, I've only ever loved you."

"How could the Colony poison your thoughts?" She lifted her chin. "It's just a building."

"A building that my magic is linked to," he said. "If there's something wrong with it then none of this is—" He broke off, but she could sense the direction of his thoughts.

"Your fault."

"Exactly."

She stared at him until he sighed.

"You're not going to believe me, are you?" His tone was despondent and his shoulders sank just enough to make her gut clench with guilt.

"I want to." Part of her did.

"But you can't."

Her stomach clenched. She shook her head.

The silence, barbed and stinging, stretched between them. Cody stared at her, his will bombarding her along the bond, desperate for her to believe him.

She just didn't have it in her.

Not any longer.

A few minutes passed before he spoke again. "Come on. Let's get back to the camp. I'm sure you're exhausted."

"You're leaving?"

The thought made something shatter inside her. It shouldn't have because it went against all her notions of self-protection, but she'd been right, in the end.

He wouldn't stick it out.

Cody stopped and whipped around to face her. "No fucking way." His nose was an inch away from hers, his eyes hard, lush lips pressed into a firm line. "I'm not leaving you. Not ever again. If you need me I promise will *always* be there."

Her breath caught, attempting to absorb the impact of the vow he'd given her so many times before, but found herself unable to trust in it.

He took her hand, footsteps silent as he led her out of the forest.

"Someday I hope you'll believe it's the truth."

TWENTY-FIVE

DAUGHTRY CREPT DOWN THE HALL, not wanting to wake Dominic and yet unable to sleep.

As she tiptoed down the stairs, cringing at every creak of the worn wood, she tried to resolve some of the mass of emotions within her. Despite everything that was going on with Cody, that wasn't what was keeping her awake.

No, it was the persistent niggling within her mind that prevented her from sleeping. The feeling that she was missing something, that there were pieces about her past she needed to discover.

She stepped gingerly across the family room and into the kitchen.

Chocolate. What she needed was two cubic tons of the stuff.

She reached into the freezer for the frozen variety—

"Whatcha doing?"

Shrieking, she bonked her head on the open door when Dominic's voice came from directly behind her ear.

"Oh careful," he said, steadying her shoulders.

"Careful?" she asked, her voice shrill. "Careful?" Turning

around, she glared at him then shoved him hard. "How about you don't sneak up on someone like that?"

Dominic didn't stumble, didn't even shift one inch backward. Instead, his lips curled up and he snagged her hand.

Something about the movement was familiar.

The memories surged up and pulled her under—

"You're not my mom." She saw a younger version of herself— maybe eight—tell Judith. They were in the middle of a supermarket, bananas on one side, apples on the other. She and Thomas had been joking around, filling the cart full of fruit and treats just a few seconds before.

Then the truth had pierced through Daughtry's mind.

Judith's eyes darted around the almost empty store before focusing back on Daughtry with narrowed intent. "Of course I am, sweetheart." Anyone listening would have thought the endearment genuine.

Daughtry knew different.

The slight snap of Judith's Ts, the pulled-down brows, the disappearing lips. All of those spelled trouble later for Daughtry. Trouble that came in the form "missed" meals and days without being allowed from her room.

But she couldn't let this pass. It was important for her to remember, to hang onto the dredges of the memories from her life before.

"You're not!"

It was a piercing shriek. One that took Thomas and Judith both by surprise.

"You're not my mother!"

Judith glanced at Thomas and there might have been fear instead of fury in her expression. "Take her out to the car."

At the order, at Thomas's hand on her shoulder, everything in Daughtry snapped.

She wrenched away and tried to run.

Judith's hands stopped her and she began screaming. For someone to help her, that Judith wasn't her mother, that everything was wrong.

After a moment's hesitation, Judith recovered.

Her voice became joking, her fingernails little needle pricks into Daughtry's upper arms. "Oh dear, someone's tired. Let's go, sweetheart." Another painful squeeze.

Slowly, Daughtry was pulled from the store, the full cart forgotten right in the middle of the produce section.

She tried to fight, really she did.

In the end it didn't matter. Less than a minute later, she was in the back of the car, screeching from the lot.

Later, when they got home, after she'd exhausted herself pounding on the locked door of her bedroom, after she'd collapsed into a heap of rubbery limbs and tear-stained cheeks, Thomas knocked quietly.

"Daughtry?" his soft voice came through the door.

She didn't answer, didn't bother. Because she already knew what he was going to say.

"She's coming." Her life would be snatched away, every bit of those precious memories she'd clung to, would be lost once again.

Hot tears fell anew—

The vision faded away and Daughtry found herself slumped onto the kitchen floor.

Dominic must have turned the lights on, she realized, blinking against the glaring fluorescent lights. He sat next to her, his arm touching hers, some small gesture that she would like to believe was his attempt at not allowing her to be alone—even when mired within the depths of her own mind.

"What'd you see this time?"

Her eyes shot up, locked onto Dominic's almost black ones. "What?" She shook her head. "How—I've had them before?"

He nodded. "You weren't here for long, less than a year. Do you remember spending time with me? With Brigette?"

"I remember Brigette, or portions of our interactions. You . . . I'm not sure. You feel comfortable, I guess. Even though my brain can't pull any memories up." She hadn't remembered Dominic at all when he'd first stopped her in the forest, but she couldn't deny the sense of familiarity with the Forgotten's camp, with Brigette and the surrounding area. And with him.

"Here." He shoved something cardboard into her palm. It was the journal Brigette had given her.

She paged through it, looking at her scribbles, at the disjointed thoughts. The only recurring theme she could identify was an overwhelming sense of wrongness. It had grown over the months, tearing at her happiness, locking her into a cycle of confusion and red-hot anger.

That hadn't changed, Daughtry realized.

The blocks must have been reinforced after her time with the Forgotten, after the episode in the grocery store. But that hadn't made her forget.

Not completely.

Probably she should feel violated and distraught that someone had so thoroughly destroyed the sanctity of her mind. And though those thoughts *were* laced into her emotions, the driving feeling in her mind was pride.

Daughtry *hadn't* forgotten. She had fought the blocks.

Which meant she was a hell of a lot stronger than she gave herself credit for.

If nothing else came of her time here with the Forgotten, at least she could hold on to that.

"COME WITH ME."

"Huh?" Her eyes shot up, focused on Dominic's face. She'd been lulled into a sort of peaceful wakefulness—not quite numb, not quite sleeping, just zoning as she attempted to tease out more of her memories.

The images that crossed her psyche weren't as well formed as her shouting match in the grocery store, but they did fill in some of the gaping holes within her.

Daughtry hadn't realized how much it had affected her, the not knowing. But having evidence that spoke to her strength, instead of the failures, instead of her weakness in trying to please her kidnappers—that was valuable and so fucking important.

He grinned at her then grabbed up her hand and pulled her to her feet.

"Come with me."

They were out the door a few seconds later, Daughtry stumbling to keep up with Dominic's rapid pace.

The path was dark, the night air crisp, the space surrounding them quiet. She could smell the moist soil, the delicate floral scent of the night-blooming flowers, the soft *hoot* of an owl in the distance. All the houses that encircled the clearing were dark. Including the one Dominic stopped in front of.

He let go of her hand to stoop and pick up something off the ground.

Before she could ask what he was doing, he placed the object in her hand.

A pebble?

"Do it," he whispered.

The small rock barely weighed anything in her palm. It was cold, smooth, and dark as night in the minimal night.

"Do what?" she asked.

Warm fingers closed over hers. "Remember," Dominic said. "Then *do it*."

"You know that you're not making any sense, right?"

White teeth flashed bright. "Remember."

A bolt of irritation went straight through Daughtry. She wanted to tell Dominic that he and all of his vague *remembers* could suck it.

She didn't.

Instead, her eyes slid closed and she focused her awareness on the space around her, the familiar weight of the pebble in her palm, the calming feeling of the cool breeze on her cheeks, ruffling her hair.

Bits and pieces began flowing into her mind, the past, the present all mixed together. She *had* stood in that very spot before. Many times, in fact. She and Dominic and Brigette had snuck out several times a week during Daughtry's stay here.

Well, *she* had snuck out. Brigette and Dominic had been adults, able to move about the Forgotten's camp without consequence.

And yet they'd kept up the charade.

She would climb out her window, meet up with Dominic and then they'd take turns throwing pebbles at Brigette's window.

Dominic always missed.

And she—

Had used magic to direct the rock into just the right spot.

If someone had touched her at that moment, she would have probably fallen straight over.

"We're going to miss it," Dominic murmured.

Miss what, she wasn't sure. Because the truth was rocketing through her. Had she really—*really?*—used her powers without consequence before?

Deciding to alter Kaitlin's vision had been the most difficult thing she'd ever done because she'd thought her magic damaged, tainted. The trust and confidence she'd gained as a result of changing the little girl's future for the better had been huge.

Now to learn that she'd done magic in such a happenstance way, added another layer to that faith.

Despite the fact that her memories were Swiss cheese, that she was frustrated having spent so long not even knowing her magic had existed. Despite the fact that someone had stolen the memories and ability from her, it was good news.

She wasn't broken.

She also wasn't stupid. The first sign that something was wrong and she would lock her powers right back up in the iron-clad box within her mind.

Because a lot had happened in the years since her younger self had stayed here.

Though Daughtry wasn't Dalshie, wasn't tainted with black magic, she also wasn't entirely convinced that she was out of the woods yet. She worried if she let her guard down, went all in with her powers, that she'd miss the signs and she'd slide down the slippery slope that had led all previous Oracles to the dark side of magic.

So though she'd seen evidence of her younger self using her powers without them ramping out of control, caution was still the name of the game.

But it *was* nice to have hope again.

"How do I do it?" How did she use her magic to direct the rock?

"You'll figure that out."

A snort. "You're too helpful."

"It's a gift." His mouth quirked. "It's *that* window."

A smile tugged at her lips, and amusement filled her from head to feet. "I know that much."

Pulling on the faint impression of memories, Daughtry called on her magic. It was a pathetically thin strand, barely visible to the eye, but she held on to it, allowed it to ball itself into a sphere on her palm. Then she waited for the urge to grab more of her magic, to let her powers overwhelm her and bleed out into the space around her. For a long time, she simply focused inward, and watched.

Then, eventually, when nothing spun out of control, no flames burst forth to singe the area, she allowed instinct to guide her.

The thread of violet magic curled around the pebble, wrapping it as tight as a ribbon on a Christmas present.

It took more mental strength than she would have expected to lift it from her palm, to throw it through the air.

It flew about six feet before falling to the ground.

Dominic chuckled. "You're out of practice."

She could feel the sweat starting to bead on her scalp, to sheen her skin. The night suddenly wasn't as cold. She glared at him then bent to pick up another pebble.

This time she pulled more magic, a thicker strand, wrapped the rock tighter.

It cleared the distance to Brigette's window easily then collided with a sharp *rap*. They both winced at the noise.

A second later the light went on and the window opened.

"Are you kidding me?" Brigette's head poked out, anger marring the delicate features of her face.

That is, until she saw it was Dominic and Daughtry. Then she grinned. "I'll be right down."

The room went dark and thirty seconds later Brigette was standing in front of them.

"I can't go far. Laila is asleep," she said.

Dominic nodded, tilted his head in the direction of the forest.

"You left the window open," he said. "We'll be within shouting distance. Laila makes a peep, we'll hear it."

He led the way, Brigette and Daughtry trailing him. It was less than a minute later when they stopped.

"Oh," she said, her feet sliding to a stop, eyes taking in what was in front of her. The memory of her first time seeing the beautiful bioluminescence of the pond merged with witnessing it through her adult gaze.

It was even more gorgeous after having seen so much death and destruction, so much pain and suffering.

Sinking down at the water's edge, she ran her fingers lightly through the surface. The little creatures that lived within the pond were bright in the dark night.

"I'd forgotten this was here," she murmured.

"I know," Dominic said, as he and Brigette sank down next to her.

"Do you remember the first time you saw it?" Brigette asked.

Daughtry nodded. They'd taken her here in an effort to cheer her up. She'd been so distraught, so saddened by something that Judith had said.

She couldn't even recall the exact insult now, because the sense of her being so small, so meaningless in the huge world, had been dwarfed by the fact that such tiny organisms could make such a large effect.

It had been awe-inspiring as a child. As an adult, it wasn't much different.

"You do pep talks better than anyone I knew, Dominic," she said.

He smiled at her, his teeth appearing green from the reflected light. "I do what I can."

The three of them sat in silence for a long time. Hope for the future, to regain the past, to continue their friendship woven between them.

For the first time in a long time, Daughtry didn't feel so alone.

TWENTY-SIX

SHE PUSHED BACK the covers and stood. Sunlight streamed in through the windows of Dominic's cabin, illuminating dust motes, dappling across the carpeting. After tugging on the pair of sweats that Brigette had loaned her, she scraped her hair into a ponytail.

So much for her plan to be out of there before the sun rose.

After stepping into her shoes, she opened the door. It creaked loudly but that wasn't what made her heart jump.

Cody stood against the opposite wall, arms crossed. His biceps bulged below the sleeves of his T-shirt, his abs were flat, and his face was scruffy.

In other words, he was the picture of the man who'd stolen her heart. Right down to the softening in his emerald eyes as she approached him.

Her gaze dropped to the floor as she drew in a steadying breath. It didn't hurt quite as much as the day before. She'd lain in bed long after midnight, analyzing what he'd told her.

"Will you come with me?"

The question had her head jerking up. Cody didn't make requests. Not ever. That he was doing so now—

She shook her head, trying to clear her thoughts, and felt a burst of frustration—of helplessness—streak toward her along the bond.

"No. I mean. Yes." Her hand chopped down, cutting them both off. "What I mean is yes, I'll go with you. No, to the thought in my head."

His lips twitched. "Okay." He started to reach for her hand then stopped and gestured her forward. "After you."

They walked down the stairs and into the kitchen. Dominic sat at the round wooden table, laptop open, a stack of papers to the left of it. "Morning," she said.

"Morning," he responded, the tone absent. He spared her a glance, eyes warm until they tracked to a spot over her shoulder, presumably Cody standing behind her. His expression cooled. "I thought I told you to leave her alone. How'd you even get in here anyway?"

Cody shrugged, a wide smirk revealing bright white teeth. "I'm resourceful." A beat. "And you couldn't keep me out, even if you tried."

Dominic stood. "I—"

"Are we going somewhere?" she said to interrupt the testosterone fest.

Cody held up a bag, the smirk fading, his expression cautious. "I hope so."

"Fine," she said. "Let's go." She turned to Dominic. "I'll be back soon. I'd like to talk to Brigette and Laila before I leave."

"Of course." He hesitated. "You know that you don't have to leave."

She glanced over her shoulder, touched the mental connection linking her with Cody. "I think I do."

If she didn't face this, she'd be running forever.

It wasn't that she was softening to Cody. Not really.

No, it was because moving forward was on her. She was tired of running from her magic, from Cody.

At the very least, she needed to come to terms with all the hurt and concentrate on the future.

Her past wouldn't hold her back. Not any longer.

She had started for the back door before she remembered the other half of the equation that had kept her up the previous evening. She turned back. "Have you spoken to Seth?"

"Not yet," Dominic said. "But this is early for him. I suspect he'll be sleeping for a few more hours." He sat back down. "Go on. I'd say have fun, but that doesn't appear possible with that one."

"Cody?" she asked, affecting innocence. "No, he's just misunderstood."

Annoyance slammed into her and she glanced over at her bondmate, silently dared him to say something.

He didn't, instead just held the back door open for her.

At the bottom of the stairs he paused, but she waved him forward. "Lead the way."

As she followed in Cody's wake, observed the fluid way with which his body moved, the confident steps that ate up the ground much faster than her own, Daughtry wondered again if she could believe what he'd told her.

More than that, was she curious enough to risk shedding the barriers she'd erected in order to find out?

Caution warred with desire and not just the lust kind, either. Because Cody *was* still the same gorgeous blond-haired, green-eyed man she'd fallen in love with. His nose was straight, his jaw strong, his lips soft and kissable, but the part of him she'd always felt most attracted to was his mind.

His quick sense of humor, his intelligence. The sweet ways he'd take care of her, not just bodily but soul-deep—even going so far as to ferret the truth out of her mind in order to discover what was really wrong when she was upset.

But that didn't mean the past had changed.

Cody's ability to be in her mind meant that he had hurt her more deeply than any other person could have.

He'd taken her love and thrown it back in her face.

The frustrating thing was that a part of her wasn't even upset about it. Cody hadn't dumped her for another woman or tired of her. No, he'd done it for family.

It was noble, honorable . . . heart-breaking.

Because she'd thought *he* was her family.

In a world where she was alone, Cody had become her foundation.

That had probably been her biggest mistake.

She needed to be the concrete and rebar of her own life. Her friends could be the walls, the windows, the finishings of the home that surrounded her heart. But without a firm base— and her as that groundwork—it would simply sink into the earth.

"Your thoughts are moving too fast for me to hear, but I don't like the emotions I'm feeling," Cody said, looking at her over his shoulder, the words so soft that she almost didn't hear them.

"Oh," she said, stopping as they reached the end of the clearing. The trail was before them, lined with tall pines, the whisper of the scent of their needles combining with Cody's to soothe her. "I *want* to forgive you. So much. But *how* can I do it?" She leaned back against a tree, felt the rough bark through her shirt.

"I—"

She held up a hand. "I know you say it was the *fog* in your mind manipulating your thoughts. But the truth is, *you* said those things, not someone else." Her eyes darted to the ground and back up. "And how are we supposed to go on when Caroline hates me? When you won't stand up to her for me?"

"I will. I promise." He closed the distance between her, got to his knees. "And I will literally beg if you want me to. Just give me another chance."

She grabbed his shoulders and yanked him to his feet. "Dammit, Cody. That's not what I want."

"Then what?" he asked, sounding so lost that she felt a different kind of hurt for a change. Instead of pain for herself, it was for him.

"I–I–" The bark snagged her shirt as she sank to the ground. "I don't know. Do you really believe it was the *fog* that made you tell me all of those things? Do you really not blame me for Caroline?"

"I'm going to say this only one more time." The anger in his voice had her eyes flying up to his.

Because he sounded like himself for a change, not the cruel man who'd broken her heart or even the shattered one who'd begged just seconds before. "I do *not* blame you for Caroline." He shook his head when she would have spoken. "So what if the person who held her looked like you? That's where you're going, isn't it?"

Daughtry nodded.

"It's probably the Dalshie's way of manipulating us further, their attempt to separate us. For all we know, it's a fucking glamour."

Her heart beat a little faster. "Do you really think so?"

"It's a legitimate possibility." He shrugged. "But there's only one way for you to know my true feelings."

"What? Oh." Her throat went a little tight at his implication. He wasn't talking about the glamour any longer. He meant that the only way for her to really see if he blamed her for Caroline was to open herself up to the bond.

To expose her heart.

Could she?

"I won't pressure you," he thought. *"I made that promise before and broke it. Never again."*

The intimacy of his mind against hers was beyond nice. It filled her every cell with warmth, strengthened her, gave her hope.

"I mean it," he told her aloud, reaching out to cup her cheek for the barest second before leaning back. "Our relationship has been on my terms for too long. You've given too much. It's my turn now."

Silence stretched between them as his words pinged around in her mind, settled her racing heart, released the tension in her muscles.

Cody had once told her that she represented possibilities to him. She finally understood what he'd meant.

"If there is someone or something manipulating minds at the Colony, who could it be?"

His face darkened. "I don't know. I'm not even one hundred percent sure if it was even the Colony. It did get worse when I was there, but maybe we were wrong about Caroline, maybe she's turned—"

"She hasn't." Daughtry's spidey-sense for the Dalshie had told her that much at least.

"I won't ask if you're sure."

"I am," she said and felt her chin lift. Her instincts hadn't failed her yet.

His eyes flashed with humor but his voice was soft. "Thanks." For not condemning his sister, despite how awful Caroline had been. "Have *you* sensed anything at the Colony?"

Daughtry knew that Cody's real concern was that there could be another hidden Dalshie there—like the woman who'd posed as Caroline had been. She'd glamoured herself so effectively, managed to hide her true nature so well that no one suspected anything.

A shake of her head. "I don't think so. I always felt that there was something off with Caro—I mean *that* woman—I just ignored it. I haven't felt anything like that with anyone else."

But she'd been away from the Colony a lot in recent weeks. Had she missed some sign?

"Okay." He fell silent, the thoughts churning along his side of the bond.

It was tempting, so tempting, to open their connection fully, to allow herself to read those thoughts. She could just let loose the hold she had on her mind, her heart. Let it join with Cody's—

"What's in the bag?" she asked before she could give into the urge.

His head flew up. "What?"

"The bag? Is it your latest fashion accessory statement piece or something else?"

"Hilarious," he grumbled. "Here." He handed her a container. "Breakfast." A shrug. "Kind of."

"Oh." Her heart squeezed. Cookies, the misshapen circles almost certainly made by hand. She could almost feel the love for her pouring off them.

Or maybe that was just coming across the bond.

He shrugged again. "It's nothing," he said, before plunking a soda can into her hand.

She cleared her throat and blinked back tears—happy ones for a change.

"Don't do that," he said quickly, putting up a palm as if it might stop her from crying. "It's just soda."

"And chocolate," she said. The cookies rattled around in the container as she struggled to contain the emotions flooding through her. Numbness was a thing of the past. The huge feelings Cody evoked had returned full force. "You made them?"

"Laila helped me." His expression was that of a sheepish schoolboy. It unlocked the last bit of her reticence. "I'm going to do better," he told her. "I don't want to be separated. Not ever again."

The words washed over her, giving her the courage to do what she'd been resisting.

She let the barriers around her heart fall to the wayside.

TWENTY-SEVEN

HER MAGIC SURGED along the bond, free at last, desperate to connect with Cody's. She watched in amazement as it healed the fragile connection of their minds, turned the pale, brittle strands into thick ropes of deep purple.

Cody's emerald magic rose in suit, meeting hers more than halfway. It flowed into her mind, spread through her limbs, settled over her skin.

The connection had always been like that, a warm blanket, the very description of home and comfort.

Impossible to resist.

She could hear his every thought, feel his every emotion. And there were a lot of them.

Love. Hope. Fear. Disappointment. Affection.

A whirling, swirling snowstorm of feelings.

When the bond had settled, retreated again into the background of her mind, she opened her eyes.

Cody stood before her, his mouth open, arms limp at his sides.

"Why did you—?"

"You've never understood your appeal, have you?" She patted his cheek. *"You were right. I needed to see for myself."*

It was . . . like coming home to talk to him that way, to have his magic interlaced with her own. They were the flip sides of the same coin. He the healer. She the killer. Their powers were polar opposites and in that, the universe found balance.

"You're not a killer."

Her lips curved up into what was probably a pathetically small smile. "Tell that to my past." She continued before he could contradict her. "But with the success of Kaitlin, I hope that—maybe—I can change that.

"You're perfect," he said, eyes intense as he bent to meet her own. "Just the way you are."

"And you're laying it on thick," she told him.

"Daughtry." A warning.

One she didn't heed. *"Cody."*

"You don't see yourself clearly."

She rolled her eyes. "I've said it before but I'll say it again. Pot meet kettle."

His sigh was that of a man who knew this battle was lost. Smart one that he was, Cody changed the subject. "Who's Seth?"

She sank back against the tree, the soil soft, almost springy beneath her. It was a surprisingly comfortable seat.

Exhaustion had soaked into her limbs, making them heavy and almost useless. Using her magic always tired her and today was no different. She might have not actively called it forth, but unconscious use or not, her body still needed time to recover.

"Seth is Dominic's brother," she said then shook her head. "Well, he's Dominic's friend, but the Forgotten consider each other family because of everything they've been through."

The lid of the plastic container she still held in her hands made a popping noise as she pulled it off. When the cookie hit her tongue, a sigh slipped between her lips.

Medicating with chocolate. Now *that* was what she needed.

Cody sat next to her, shoulder to shoulder, thigh to thigh.

"Tell me the truth." At her words, he looked over sharply. "Laila did most of the work, didn't she?"

Cody smirked. "That's remarkably sexist of you."

"Don't think I haven't noticed that you didn't answer."

"Fine," he grumbled. "Make a guy tell you all of his secrets. I added the eggs." He mock-flexed. "And these arms were a requirement for the stirring."

She laughed, wrapped up in his amusement across the bond, enjoying the little slice of how things used to be.

The sounds of the forest washed over her. It was noisy, much more so than she might have expected. Birds called in the distance. Children screamed as they played somewhere nearby. Even the squirrels were loud as they knocked pinecones and branches to the ground.

It took her a few minutes to recognize that Cody didn't share her relaxed attitude. "What's the matter?"

"Nothing." He shook his head when she raised a brow. "Okay, not *nothing*. My instincts are screaming at me."

"*Screaming* what exactly?"

He pushed to his feet and paced away. "I'm missing something important. My mind won't shut down. There's this persistent niggling that something's not right." His feet ate up the distance between the trees then back toward her and he came close enough to grasp her shoulders. "I ignored my instincts the first time my powers manifested, the first time I ever saw a Dalshie. I felt the same damned way then as I do now. But I ignored it and I don't want the same thing to happen—"

The words cut off abruptly as Cody closed his mouth.

Daughtry rose too. "What? When you were . . . "

"I—" A shudder tore through his body.

"Hey." She touched his arm. "What is it?"

Images flew across his mind, too fast for her to comprehend. She'd see a flash of color then nothing. Like Cody was trying to delete the pictures before they made their way to her consciousness.

His breath puffed in and out. "I'm sorry. I–uh–" *"I'm not usually this weak."*

That Cody was reacting this way scared her. He was always so composed. To see him this agitated—sucked into the choke-hold of the past—humbled her.

He wasn't infallible. He was human. Or the sort of human-plus that the Rengalla were. But being near immortal didn't mean that one didn't make mistakes.

God knew she'd made plenty.

Their peace was fragile. New. *This* bolstered it. Daughtry knew she wasn't perfect, and it was time she accepted he wasn't either. For the first time, she owned up to her part of their conflict. Cody wasn't the only bad guy.

She had avoided rather than risk putting herself on the line and pushing back. She'd been a coward, afraid to fight for him, for their relationship.

That put things in perspective.

"I don't blame you for staying away." His fingers clenched into fists.

"I do," she said. "I promised to give us my best chance then ran off at the first hurt feelings. I should have pushed back." Her bangs hung in her face and she scraped them to the side. "Deep down, a part of me knew that wasn't you, that you wouldn't do or say those things. But I was too scared to fight." A sigh. "Which is completely pathetic."

"Fuck that," Cody scoffed. "I was an asshole and pushed exactly the right buttons to distance you."

"You *were* really good at that."

"It's a gift." Sarcasm, but at his own expense.

She wondered who was pulling the strings, who'd messed with Cody's mind, and how or why despite their link, she hadn't sensed the manipulation. If they didn't find out who—

One step at a time.

First her and Cody. Then all the rest of it.

"You going to tell me what memory still cuts at you? Or I can . . ." She tapped her temple. It had been easier for Cody to delve into some of the memories of her past, easier to not have to regurgitate them aloud.

"No." His answer was abrupt. "It's too . . . much to remember in detail. Can I just tell you?"

"You don't have to." It was a little late to make that claim, but part of her hesitated. She didn't want to hurt him. And how awful were the memories that he didn't want her to see?

The thought made her pulse pound, her tongue dry. Except . . . they'd come this far and if they were to have a future, it had to exist in complete honesty.

"Can we walk and talk?" he asked.

"When did you start making requests?"

Cody wasn't the type of man to force his prerogative onto another person, but he also didn't make allowances that were unnecessary. In all their time together, he'd never asked her so many questions.

"A bit of a role reversal, is it?" He smiled but his eyes still held the sadness of the past, the present. "I'm trying to not be pushy."

"Pushy is okay in some things," she said. "*Like bed.*" Her cheeks heated at the thought.

Of course Cody noticed as well.

His smile turned into a smirk. "Noted." He paused, weighing her emotions. "This way."

"Atta boy," she said, just to wipe that annoying little curl of his lips off his face.

It didn't work. "I'd say that you were going to pay for that," Cody said. "But I don't think you will."

"Noted. Still, I think I can get away with snotty comments for awhile."

"You're hilarious."

The path they took was well worn, wide enough for them to walk side by side. He slanted a glance towards her. "You already know that I was a Null as a child. But do you know what that really means?"

"Caroline—er, that woman—said it meant that you didn't have magic." Daughtry paused. "But that's not possible. I've seen your powers, they're coursing through me right now."

Cody glanced at her. "That's true. I have magic now and it's even stronger because of the bond. As a five—and a six, seven, and eight—year old, that wasn't the case."

He laced his fingers with hers and held tight. The warmth of his hand centered her.

She hoped her touch did the same for him.

"The oldest on record for a child's powers to emerge when I was tested was eight years old." A self-deprecating smile curled his lips. "I screwed the curve on that one. I was twenty-four when my magic first appeared."

Daughtry would have made a joke if not for the seriousness of his emotions along the bond. His attempt to corral the memories had pulled their link taut, almost painfully so.

"I was surrounded by Dalishe, chained by my arms and legs, the first time my magic appeared."

A gasp escaped her lips. "My God. How did—?" She shook her head, trying to focus. "How did the Dalshie find you?"

Cody swallowed. "I remained in the system—at the same orphanage my parents dropped me off at until I was eighteen.

When I was old enough to be on my own, I began searching for the Rengalla." She felt the bond shudder under the weight of his memories. "I wanted my old life."

His stride faltered, and he pulled her to stop then wrapped his arms around her. "But an eight-year-old doesn't exactly have a good grasp of geography. I didn't know how to get home. Only that I wanted to."

As he talked, images began to creep across the bond—

Cody had left the orphanage with only the clothes on his back, his coat torn and threadbare, his shoes too small. He was thin, painfully so.

Daughtry watched months speed by, a vignette of his searches, felt his disappointment as every lead failed to bring forth more information about the Rengalla.

Years passed. Cody worked a series of jobs—dock worker, ice deliverer, stable mucker. He was surviving but he wasn't whole.

Because he wasn't home. He missed the easy life of the Colony. He missed his friends. He thought that if he found his way back to the Rengalla, his parents would finally accept him.

"What happened?" she whispered, afraid to disrupt Cody's thoughts.

The images in her mind shifted, fast-forwarding.

He held a slip of paper, an address that was supposed to lead him to someone who could do magic. He'd paused on the street, gut screaming, instincts telling him not to go inside.

He'd gone anyway.

They could do magic.

It was just the wrong kind.

The warehouse was secluded, a squat gray brick building on the edge of town. And inside—a group of four Dalshie waited for him.

They chained him to the wall.

Her mind was locked with his. She could feel the painful

clamp of the manacles around his wrists, feel every blow they unleashed on his body. First it had just been the Dalshie's fists, knocking the wind out of him, breaking his nose, his eye socket. Then it was their feet.

Cody's arms burned from being held above his head. His ribs were in agony from the repeated blows from booted feet.

That was when they pulled out their knives.

Daughtry had seen them before. Jagged black blades that almost seemed to absorb the blood of their victim.

Cody was no different.

His screams of pain riddled the room, echoed off the walls.

He knew he was going to die before the Dalshie drew the blade across his throat.

Except his blood didn't splatter, didn't spurt to the bare dirt floor. It froze in place, remained in the severed veins and arteries.

Something strained in his mind. Stretched.

The cruel malice of the Dalshie enraged him. His nerves burned and—

Snap.

Hot power slid down his spine. It healed his neck before shooting out his palms.

The bright emerald strands were razor sharp.

They sliced through the Dalshie in front of him, reciprocating the wound the monster had tried to inflict on Cody. From there they whipped around the room, cornering and ashing the remaining Dalshie.

Flecks of dust coated Cody's bloodied skin, floated through the room.

He was too exhausted to free himself, to move, to do anything further to save his own life.

Regardless of the commotion at the far side of the room.

A man walked in—John, she realized with a gasp. He was followed by two men that Daughtry didn't recogn—

"Cowgirl."

She blinked and pulled back into her own mind. Her body was trembling, the burn of Cody's remembered wounds leaving almost real marks on her consciousness, her skin.

"You're shaking." He tightened his hold on her and she leaned into the strength of his broad chest. "I was trying to make it so you didn't have to see that."

"I'm fine," she said. "I sort of got sucked in." An inhale of air as she breathed in his pine and sea salt scent. "Plus, you've seen all of my bad memories, it's only fair for me to see some of yours."

He huffed out a laugh and she couldn't imagine the years of loneliness, the frustrated helplessness that had been Cody's life.

"What did your parents say when John brought you home?"

One of his brows went up. "What do you think they said?"

So his welcome hadn't gone as he'd hoped. Her heart squeezed for the pain he'd endured. "Not even after they learned about your powers?"

He shrugged. "It wasn't *all* their fault. I wasn't ready to make amends."

"I don't blame you. They abandoned you over something that you had no control over. Why make the effort to get them to like you?"

"Exactly." The word puffed over her hair, tickled her nape. "Plus I had John and Dante."

Cody began to say something else, except shouting erupted behind them. They both turned in the direction of the clearing, ears straining to make out the conversation.

She put a hand on his chest, staying him when he would have taken off in the direction.

"I'm sure it's nothing," she said. "Probably just Seth arguing with Dominic again. They got pretty loud yesterday about Seth's attempt to sell me to the Dalshie."

TWENTY-EIGHT

"PLEASE TELL me that you're kidding," Cody said.

His eyes were wide, his body stiff, ready for an attack.

For the first time Daughtry considered that perhaps she should have led with the whole giving-her-to-the-Dalshie-and-collecting-the-finder's-fee portion of yesterday's activities.

She'd been too torn up to think properly and now—

"Dominic told him no," she said.

Cody snorted.

"The Forgotten ran from the Dalshie. They won't work with them."

"The life of one for the lives of many," Cody muttered then grabbed her hand and began to lead her parallel to the clearing. "People can be motivated to do some pretty gruesome things in order to save their own skin." A pause. "Or those they love."

He lifted her over a fallen log before pulling her forward at a fast clip.

"Where are we going?" she asked, stumbling in her efforts to keep up.

"There's a road on the opposite side of the clearing. And a garage. We're getting the hell out of here."

Daughtry followed him without complaint. Her own instincts were prickling. She just wished she hadn't left the journal Brigette had given her—

"I have it."

"What?"

Cody had the grace to look sheepish. "I cleared out your room this morning." He shrugged at the glare she gave him. "What? Instincts remember?"

"Yeah," she said. *"With just a hint of nosiness."*

"Maybe." He paused. *"I didn't read it."*

"I know." *"Thanks."*

The journal was another piece of the puzzle, one she hadn't yet fully absorbed. But since it was a new piece, it was still a little raw, like she was exposing a vulnerable part of herself to the world.

If Cody had taken advantage of that by reading the diary, it would have hurt her deeply—just when their trust was beginning to rebuild.

"Did you get here in a car?" *"Can we bypass the camp and head straight for it?"*

Cody nodded. "It's parked off the road only four miles to the east. But if the Dalshie are close or coming, we can't count on it still being there." He held a branch out of the way for her then guided her through a series of thick underbrush. "But we can't risk not having a car."

"Couldn't they track that?"

"Maybe. But hopefully we'll be long gone before they realize it. We'll dump it somewhere and get something else."

Daughtry gave a pained gasp when a thorny branch from a bush cut her arm. "Why don't we just call Morgan?" she asked, holding her hand to the cut.

Cody peeled her palm away and touched the small hurt with his own. His magic washed over her, healing the cut.

"Thanks," she said.

"Anytime." He ducked under a low hanging limb. "We can't call Morgan because I don't have a phone."

There was that.

"What happened to yours?" she asked, remembering the way her own phone had cracked thanks to her affinity for tripping.

"Threw it at Dante's head."

She started to laugh then realized he was serious. "Why? Why would you do that?"

"Because he kept trying to stop me from coming. Wanted to follow procedure." She came up alongside him. The voices coming from the clearing had quieted and she wondered what had happened. Was it actually about her or were they overreacting? "I wouldn't listen."

"Procedure is there for a reason."

"I know."

"And you still threw the phone?"

"I was pissed," he said. "Told him he'd have to lock me in the cells in the basement to stop me from going after you. Then I got in a car and started driving."

The trees began thinning and their path opened up. A gray building sat in front of them.

"The garage?" she thought.

He nodded. *"The keys are in a box at the front of the building. Stay here while I grab a set."*

Before she could argue, he was gone.

His movements were nearly impossible to track. The slightest rustling of a bush here, the soft *squeak* of hinges as the door opened. But even with the dappled daylight, Cody used cover and shadows to his advantage.

He might as well have been an apparition.

"Got 'em." She heard the door close quietly, sensed him getting nearer, a growing presence on her right side.

She started to rise, ready to get away from the Forgotten before her being there brought them trouble.

Her foot was raised in anticipation of climbing over a log that was in her way, when she heard it.

The bloodcurdling scream from the clearing tore through her.

"Daughtry, no!"

Cody's words didn't register.

Because Daughtry knew to whom that scream belonged.

Laila.

She ran.

CODY CAUGHT her before she reached the clearing.

"Let me go," she hissed, trying to shrug out of the hand that stopped her. Her skin burned, and a herd of elephants might as well have been stampeding around in her stomach.

Dalshie were near.

"Stop." It was a harsh command, followed by a strong mental slap. *"Think."* "You'll get us both killed running in there like that."

Panic made her mind blurry, her breathing too rapid. She needed to—

No. Cody was right. They needed to slow down. See what they were dealing with. If her instincts about the Dalshie were correct, then they needed to have a plan.

"Okay." She closed her eyes, took a breath. "I'm calm now." *"Sorry."*

His arm wrapped around her shoulders and pulled her close for a quick hug. *"It's okay,"* he told her. *"We're fine."*

When he let her go, his fingers reached up to her ponytail and gave it a quick tug. "Remember. Don't be sorry, be smart."

"Dante?" she asked.

"No." He smiled. "Shockingly that piece of wisdom came from Tyler."

Her amusement faded. She hadn't seen Tyler since he'd helped bring Caroline to the infirmary. But even before then his visits had been sparse. Her recovery after the Dalshie kidnapped them had taken longer than his and by the time she'd been sprung from the infirmary, he'd been back on LexTal rotation, accompanying John on his various missions outside the Colony.

"Is he okay?" she whispered as Cody led her backwards a few dozen feet and then clockwise around the clearing.

"He's fine. Been back at the Colony for a few weeks." He moved them closer to the ring of trees surrounding the Forgotten's camp. *"Quiet now, I think I hear someone ahead."*

She went silent but couldn't stop the little pang of guilt from traveling through her. Tyler was back and she hadn't seen him. Hadn't even known.

Was he mad he'd gotten injured and kidnapped because of her?

Was he under the same influence Cody had been?

The questions faded into the background of her mind when she saw what lay in front of them.

Dalshie—more than a dozen—surrounded a small group of the Forgotten, Laila, Brigette, and Dominic included.

Laila and Brigette seemed unhurt but Dominic was on his knees, a wound above his eyebrow bleeding freely.

"Get away."

Daughtry and Cody both jumped at the voice in their heads. Because it wasn't either of theirs.

It was Dominic's.

Cody spoke first.

"How can you hear us?" Because their telepathic communications had always been shielded. Because no one had ever been able to hear them, to eavesdrop on them before.

"It's not like I want to hear them," Dominic thought as he gave a mental shrug. *"I just can."*

Cody drew them back a few steps and squatted behind a tree. "You haven't had any visions?"

She shook her head, understanding where he was going. "I haven't seen anything. Well, that's not true. I remembered something from my past at Brigette's house, but no visions."

"I think we should leave."

"We can't!" she hissed. "Laila, Brigette, Dominic. We can't let them be hurt because of me."

"I don't want to risk you," he countered. "What if the bond is failing? What if you get more visions?"

Her throat went tight at the thought and her already churning stomach clenched.

"It's not," she said to herself, to Cody. "Dominic told me that he only hears projected thoughts. I can feel that the bond is fine. My shield is intact. It's dumb luck that no one has heard us before." He didn't look convinced, so she pressed on. "I've already been touched dozens of times here. The Forgotten aren't a risk to me."

"You can't know that." His eyes were concerned, the frown between them intense. "We don't have time to argue about it, anyway. The Dalshie surely have scouts. We need to get out, now."

Her hand on his arm stilled his efforts to herd her back into the forest. "You know we can't leave them."

"Then what, cowgirl?" he asked, exasperation making him snap the question. "Twelve against two are terrible odds."

"You'll just have to trust me."

TWENTY-NINE

"I DON'T LIKE THIS PLAN," Cody hissed.

"Is this the point that I remind you to trust me?" she asked.

They were creeping forward, Cody using his military training to scan for the enemy, Daughtry her internal Dalshie detector.

The problem with her instincts was that they were overwhelmed. With so many Dalshie in the area, she only got an all-encompassing sense of foreboding, the persistent feeling that ants were crawling underneath her skin. It was impossible to pinpoint their location with any accuracy.

Cody's skills were infinitely more helpful.

His arm snaked around her waist, halted her. "Careful now," he whispered, the words hardly a puff of air.

She glanced up, staring in the direction he nodded. Two Dalshie were positioned along the trail they'd hoped to take into the clearing—a barely used footpath that Daughtry had recalled from somewhere deep within in her memories.

Cody had tried hailing Dominic several times telepathically but he hadn't responded. Either he was out of range or he was de—

A hand pushed her towards the tree, pressed her back against the trunk. "Get down."

"What are you going to do?"

"Draw them in." His emerald eyes were full to the brim with unrestrained fury. Knowing more about the circumstances of Cody's past made her understand better why the Dalshie evoked such rage within him. "Eliminate them. Stay," he said and started to turn away then froze and added, "Please."

"Okay."

Daughtry would like to think of herself as smart, which generally meant she didn't intentionally put herself in harm's way—the last quarter hour excluded. But that aside, she knew Cody had skills she didn't, could ensure their safety better than her.

She wasn't willing to do something stupid that put them both at risk.

At the same time she wouldn't sacrifice someone else so that she could live.

Cody saw into her mind, knew her. He also knew that if he were in trouble she would jump in to save him. No matter the enemy. No matter the circumstance.

"No," he thought as he picked his way through the trees. His footsteps were silent, not the crunching of a leaf or the cracking of a branch—a predator seeking his prey.

"I won't let you get hurt," she said.

"It'll be okay, cowgirl," he said. *"This is a good plan."*

"It's a stupid plan," she said. *"We can call the Colony with coordinates from the next city over like you suggested."*

Affection drifted down the bond, warming her, settling her nerves. *"You know what I love about you, cowgirl?"* He was quiet for a heartbeat, but spoke before she could figure out a way to respond. *"You care. It's hard for me to believe sometimes, even harder to accept it."*

The notion made her choke up, squeezed the air from her lungs.

"*I don't understand how you're able to set aside every single one of my screw-ups,*" he said. "*How could I have gotten lucky enough for you to love me?*"

"*Cody—*" she began.

His next words cut her off. "*I love you, cowgirl.*"

His emotions pulsed into her, gathered in her mind, spreading into her limbs until it was an almost tangible element. The bond grew, absorbing the emotions, strengthening, becoming more durable rope than brittle vine.

"*I still think we should forget the plan—*"

He gave a mental sigh. "*There are only two of them here. Taking them out will be easy.*"

"*Let me be the judge of that.*"

"*Not a chance in hell.*" He paused, a thread of humor warming the cool notes of his mental voice. "*How about we have a safe word? One we only use in emergencies.*"

A soft laugh huffed out of her.

"*How about rhinestone cowboy?*" It was the most obscure thought bouncing around in her mind.

"*Another one of your kinky fantasies?*" Cody asked, his mental snort loud in her mind. "*Do I even want to ask?*"

Her cheeks creased in a wide smile. "*Probably not.*"

"*Okay, if I ever say 'rhinestone cowboy'—God help me if that ever happens—you can come to my rescue.*"

"*Deal.*"

"*Closing in,*" he thought, his mental voice going deadly serious. "*Quiet now.*"

Daughtry didn't respond, just focused her mind on the bond, pinpointing her attention on Cody's actions, his thoughts, and emotions.

He crept closer, skirting a pile of pine needles and stepped over a fallen branch.

With less than five feet between him and the Dalshie, he paused.

Anxiousness clawed at her, made her grip her thighs, bite her lip until she tasted blood.

She'd seen Cody fight before, but watching him stalk the Dalshie, approach them step by step was a hell of a lot different than rising to the challenge when they were ambushed.

The premeditation freaked her out.

His mind was calm, a cool catalogue of the stimuli surrounding him. The air was cold against his skin. His pulse was accelerated but steady, his body preparing for the fight to come.

Two feet now. Using a tree for cover.

He bent and removed the blade from the holster around his ankle. The leather grip was broken in, conformed exactly to his hand. It was more than just a knife, years of practice had made it an extension of his arm.

Cody rose smoothly then stepped clear of the trunk. A heartbeat later he dove at the closest Dalshie.

His aim was perfect, a smooth stroke that penetrated the Dalshie's back, piercing his heart.

Ashes.

The particles of dust clogged the air, made it difficult to see.

But he had anticipated the distraction. He lunged to the right and snagged the second Dalshie.

They hit with an impact that would have knocked the wind out of her. Instead Cody was on his knees, positioning the blade without hesitation.

He shoved hard.

The knife slipped between the Dalshie's ribs and tough connective tissue and hit home.

More ashes coated the air, sticking to Cody's face and hair. His butt fell back onto his ankles as the body beneath him disappeared.

A sigh slipped from between her lips and she sat back against the tree.

Thank God he was okay.

"*Alright*," he said, standing and brushing himself off. "*Heading back now. Stay put.*"

"*No problem.*"

The *crack* to her right had her on her feet in an instant.

"*Daughtry! Run!*"

She was already moving, lurching in the direction Cody was coming. But cold hands grabbed her and wrenched her to a stop.

Nausea made her gag. Despite the freezing fingers gripping her hard enough to leave bruises, her skin burned like it was on fire.

A malicious chuckle made her fight harder.

But there was no point.

The Dalshie holding her was stronger.

THIRTY

IN MOMENTS, Daughtry was in the clearing, surrounded by more Dalshie than she'd ever seen in her life. They dropped her on the ground, laughed when her weak legs gave out underneath her.

She struggled to her feet, her body nearly overwhelmed by the massive presence of the Dalshie surrounding her. They'd be pleased to know they wreaked havoc with her body, activating her fight-flight response, stimulating her nervous system to the point of pain.

"This was not part of the plan," Cody muttered into her mind.

His sentence was so far removed from his expected reaction that she almost laughed. She didn't, but the droll words did steady her legs, helped her keep her shoulders square, her chin raised.

Caroline emerged from the woods.

No, *not* Caroline.

Daughtry knew the malevolent look in the other woman's eyes well. It did not belong to Cody's sister. It was unique to the woman who had kidnapped her, who'd threatened to torture her friend in order to get her to cooperate.

The real Caroline might hate Daughtry, but the woman standing in front of her was infinitely more dangerous.

Her heart pounded against her rib cage, practically threatening to burst from the confines and dance around on the ground. Her fingers went cold, her legs shaky. But her voice was calm as she projected it across the clearing. "That won't work on me anymore."

Caroline's doppelgänger smiled and a buzz of magic traveled down Daughtry's spine like needles.

The glamour slipped away.

Cherry hair darkened, traversing almost the full palette of reds in its journey from fire engine to mahogany.

Green eyes changed, morphing into . . . Daughtry's personal shade of violet.

She felt strangely violated. That color was hers alone. To have this woman, this *Dalshie,* steal it chilled her to the bone.

Then the violet irises disappeared, red eyes that stared coldly at her having taken their place.

That was when the black appeared.

The markings trickled up to the woman's neck, encircling it, caressing her throat like a freakish necklace. They disappeared beneath the collar of her shirt and reappeared at her bare shoulders, before traveling down her arms to her hands.

A long skirt hid most of the woman's legs but her feet were bare. And stained black.

Daughtry could feel the bones of her jaw clenching together as she struggled to hold back her whimper. It wasn't just the color or even the markings. It was the way the gruesome tattoos writhed in excitement on the woman's—and the rest of the Dalshie's—skin.

The taint reminded her of leeches, but where the biological

version merely sucked blood, the magic version removed everything good from a person. It swapped kindness for cruelty, compassion for the thirst of power.

Horror filled her. She never wanted to become like them, would do everything in her power to avoid that fate. But today, at least, the small part of her that used to crave the blackness had fled. She felt no draw to the stain marring the woman's skin, instead all she was left with was the desire to get as far away from it as possible.

"Cody?" she thought, when it seemed like she might give into the urge to try and run.

"Stay calm," he thought. *"I'm not going anywhere."*

"Where is your *savior?*" The woman spat the word.

"I don't know who you're talking about. I came here by myself."

"Liar," the woman said. "Cody is your bondmate, he wouldn't be far from you."

"Guess again," Daughtry muttered, thinking of everything that had gone down.

A brilliant smile lit the woman's face. "It worked?" She laughed, an expression of utter delight on her face. "I can save your powers. Embrace the darkness, allow it to envelope you, to fill your soul to the very brim. It is the only thing that will prevent the loss of your magic."

"What the fuck did you do?"

Daughtry spat the question, rage filling her. She was so tired of being manipulated, of people altering *her* life by pulling the strings behind the scenes.

"Me?" She supposed the question was intended to sound innocent. But it wasn't. Not at all. "*I* didn't do anything. I believe that honor lies with your Cody." She sniffed. "What a ridiculous name for a warrior."

The laughter in her mind steadied her. *"Of everything, that's what she says?"* Cody thought. *"She's worried about my name?"*

The rage that had so filled her only moments before—the fury that would have made her stupid—was tempered by his words. It simmered now, a low, slow boil of anger that enabled her to think.

"Now, tell me where your LexTal is or more of the Forgotten will be . . . forgotten."

Daughtry glared. "Cody isn't here."

Violet eyes narrowed, a whip of black magic crackled through the air, dangerously close. "Don't bullshit me."

Daughtry swallowed, lifted her chin. "I sent him away." It was close enough to the truth that Daughtry didn't think her face would reveal the lie.

If only she had been more aware of her surroundings then she wouldn't be in this mess in the first place.

"That was stupid."

Daughtry shrugged again. "I can take care of myself."

The woman smirked. "That remains to be seen. Ah—" She pointed to a spot over Daughtry's shoulder. "Here comes my little friend now."

Seth walked into Daughtry's frame of vision. "Elisabeth," he said.

Whether it was lax security or that the Dalshie surrounding her just didn't consider him a threat, but Seth was able to pass right through the guards. He stepped up to Daughtry and wrapped an arm around her throat.

A blade pierced the skin of her neck—a bee sting of pain, a slight drip of hot blood.

She sensed across the bond that Cody was moving, but there was too much happening in front of her to process what that meant.

"I want my money," Seth said.

"Stop," Daughtry whispered, less concerned about the knife at her throat than the life of the man holding her captive.

The sound of a struggle drew everyone's eyes.

Dominic was fighting against two Dalshie, one holding each arm. "You bastard!" he screamed, throwing himself forward, causing the guards grasping him to stumble.

He slipped free from the Dalshie and sprinted for Seth. Dominic closed the distance faster than she would have thought possible, and with a quick movement of his wrist—the sickening *snap* of bone—Daughtry was free.

Seth screamed as Dominic pinned him to the ground. "How the fuck could you do this to us? To her?" He let loose a punch that made Daughtry jump back in shock then he grabbed Seth's shoulders and slammed his body against the compacted dirt.

"Stop," she said.

Dominic didn't. Just slammed Seth again, even harder than before.

"Stop!" Daughtry shouted into the mental space around her. She didn't know if it would work, if anyone besides Cody could hear her. But she had to try. *"You have to stop. He's your family."*

The telepathic hail worked.

Dominic paused, hands still on Seth's shoulders. A moment later, his fingers ratcheted open and Seth fell flat to the ground.

With a groan, Seth scrambled out of Dominic's reach and stood.

"The money," he gritted out, cradling his wrist, lip bloody and swollen, one eye already darkening.

Elisabeth smiled.

Daughtry shouted a warning, but it was too late.

The strand of black magic whipped over and cleaved Seth's head from his shoulders.

The two pieces fell to the ground, a *thump* amongst the shocked silence of the clearing.

"*That* is what will happen to the next person who crosses me." Elisabeth barely glanced at the decimated body in front of her. Instead her eyes focused on the two Dalshie guards who'd released Dominic.

Twin bolts of power burst out of Elisabeth's palms, barely making contact with the guards' skin before they exploded into ash.

"*How many left?*" Cody asked before Daughtry had even processed what had happened in front of her.

"*Eight,*" Dominic answered before she could.

"*Good. Hang tight. Stay alive for two more minutes,*" Cody told her, his words cool, almost indifferent but the emotions coursing through the bond, caressing her soul anything but. "*Cavalry's coming,*" he thought. "*When I say down, hit the deck. No questions, okay?*"

She sent a mental nod, all she could manage because Elisabeth had turned around and locked her eyes onto Dominic.

Daughtry stepped in front of him. "What do you want, Elisabeth?" she asked, pushing at Dominic when he would have moved her behind him.

"*Leave it,*" she told him. "*Elisabeth wants me too much to hurt me.*"

The other woman laughed. "What do I want?" she asked, the question laced with hysterical amusement. "A better question would be, what do I *not* want?"

Daughtry held her position, refused to cower. "You'll never get my cooperation if you harm the people around me."

Red eyes narrowed. "I seem to remember having this conversation before. I gave you what you wanted and you stabbed me in the back." A chuckle. "Or yourself in the heart. Either way, I won't make allowances this time. You'll do what I want."

"Or?" Daughtry asked.

"Or nothing." Elisabeth shrugged, a strand of magic shot over Daughtry's right shoulder and collided with Dominic's chest. He grunted, hardly a noise despite the pain that had to be coursing through him.

"Dominic?"

"I'm okay," he thought. *"Just hit me in the shoulder."*

Relief coursed through her and she forced herself to focus on what Elisabeth was saying.

"I'll take what I want. I've foreseen the future, dear Daughtry. You'll join our ranks no matter the path you chose."

"No." Daughtry didn't even recognize the harsh word that had emerged from her mouth. It was cold, razor sharp with denial.

Elisabeth laughed, a cruel, stomach-churning sound. "Not even you can alter that future." A beat. "I plan to have plenty of fun while I wait for you to traverse the path to greatness."

Another barbed, black strand flew over her head. Dominic dodged but not fast enough. The smell of singed skin hit her nostrils. He wavered, grabbing her shoulder, before managing to stagger upright.

More black magic crackled around Elisabeth, curling into the space around her, writhing in excitement. The power lurched outwards, barely tame horses rearing desperately for freedom.

Elisabeth let them sprint forward.

"Down!"

THIRTY-ONE

AT CODY'S MENTAL SHOUT, Daughtry hit the dirt hard enough to squeeze the air from her lungs. Dominic was only a half second after her.

Magic whizzed and crackled over their heads, so close that she could feel the frozen blade-like presence of it on her exposed skin.

Noise exploded around the clearing, bright flashes of light battling the strands of black. She heard Morgan's voice. Then Tyler's. John's.

The LexTals had come.

"Move," Cody told her. *"Get to the trees."*

"Let's go," Dominic said, crouching by her side, and tugging her arm when she didn't get to her feet fast enough.

His shoulder was bleeding freely, dripping down his arm, coating Daughtry's own with the warm liquid. But his pace didn't falter.

Twice he shoved her down and covered her with his body as barbed strands flew at them.

Daughtry couldn't tell if the magic coming at them was the result of an intentional attack or merely the byproduct of the

action around them, but she was grateful for Dominic's awareness, his quick actions while she was overwhelmed by the action
filling the clearing.

There was too much for her eyes to process.

The Dalshie approached the six LexTals. Dante and
Morgan's brother, Mason, had joined Cody and the others in
the scrum. Eight against six. Not bad odds if she thought
about it.

But Elisabeth tipped the balance.

Her power, her malignant presence, filled the clearing.
Magic flew from her palms freely, forced the LexTals to dodge
and block her attacks as well as fight the Dalshie coming at
them.

She and Dominic were on the wrong side of the action,
pinned against the wall of trees at their back, Elisabeth and
company in front of them.

So badly she wanted to go to Cody, to do something to help,
but knew that her lack of experience made her a liability.

The fight progressed in lurches and snail crawls. It took
John several long minutes of attack and retreat to ash one
Dalshie. Behind him, her eyes barely followed the lightning
speed of Dante as he eliminated three in quick succession, his
silver blade flashing, ash filling the air.

The particles of dust were a nuisance, but one that
impacted both sides.

Daughtry knew from experience that it clogged a person's
airways and stung their eyes. That the LexTals could keep
moving, keep fighting in spite of the obstacle humbled her.

Her successes—her desperate attempts to survive—had been
nothing but luck. A small part of her might have known that,
but the larger piece of her, the piece that had thought she could
take care of herself without issue, had just been given a boatload
of evidence to the contrary.

"Stay here." The whispered command made her eyes fly to Dominic's.

"What are you doing?" she hissed back.

"Diversion."

"Don't be stupid—" But he was already gone.

"Cody." It was the warning of a tattletale and one that probably disgusted Dominic—given the dirty look he threw over his shoulder. *"Tough,"* she told him, not about to let him go and get himself killed.

"On it," Cody answered. To Dominic he said, *"Circle left. How soon until you can create that diversion?"*

The smile in Dominic's mental voice was heady, the excitement of a male anticipating a good fight.

"Give me thirty seconds," he thought to Cody.

There were two Dalshie left, both experienced warriors by the way their blades and magic moved in tandem. Their knives and the black strands flying from their hands were extensions of their limbs. They moved in concert, a terrifyingly efficient maelstrom of magic and steel.

Combined with Elisabeth—

The LexTals could use the distraction.

Daughtry's eyes flitted around the clearing, tried to locate a weapon that might be effective against such malice. Daughtry wondered if she could—

"Don't move," Cody told her as he threw up an arm, his translucent emerald shield dispersing a bolt of black magic. *"I can't worry about you and fight."*

There was that.

"I won't," she said, worry about breaking Cody's concentration, about being the reason he was hurt—or worse—making her every muscle lock in place. Daughtry was glad for the bond because she wouldn't have been able to speak the next words without her voice cracking. *"I love you."*

An explosion drowned out any response Cody might have made.

Taking advantage of the distraction he'd known was coming, he launched himself forward, and plunged his blade into the heart of the Dalshie closest to him.

Ash coated the air, further staining his hair, his skin.

The other Dalshie was smarter or, perhaps, more experienced. He stumbled back a step as his comrade burst into nothingness.

Dante was faster.

The strand of pale gray magic ripped across the clearing, wrapped around the Dalshie's neck, and squeezed.

All that remained of the guards was ash.

A scream rent the air.

Elisabeth.

She stood, covered in black magic, a whirling storm of barbed strands, of ebony fire. Then out of nowhere, the flames banked. The wind flying through the clearing ceased.

Daughtry watched the woman who was almost her identical twin take a step towards the LexTals. Elisabeth's bare feet were silent on the smoking, charred grass, her movements as graceful as a ballerina.

One step forward. Another.

"Stop."

The order came from Dante, a terse word that had absolutely no effect on Elisabeth.

She closed the distance between herself and the LexTals.

"Stop." This time the word was from Cody. It was accompanied by the scrape of metal against metal as he pulled out another knife.

Elisabeth paused, tilted her head in almost alien fashion. "Kill him."

Daughtry was as confused as everyone else in the clearing.

Eyes darted toward each other then away, searching the trees, the space behind them for a hidden enemy.

That enemy didn't come from behind, but from beside.

From amongst their own.

While the LexTals' gazes were roving around them, Tyler raised the knife in his hand.

"Cody!" It was a mental as well as verbal scream. So loud that her mind ached and her throat felt as though a blowtorch had been taken to it.

Without conscious thought, her magic swelled, bubbled down her spine, her arms. It was pure, untainted, regulated. So different from the out of control torrent from before. Except—

Not fast enough.

Tyler's blade arched down.

But just before the knife would have penetrated Cody's back, he took one small step to the side, missed.

Her strand of magic flew between the two men, a violet javelin of power that sizzled as it collided with an overturned picnic table behind them.

Tyler raised the blade again.

"No," she whispered, horror at what was happening to her friend sending such a frigid cold down her vertebrae that she felt frozen from head to toe.

Tyler couldn't have heard the word, but sky-blue eyes met hers—no, *collided* with her stare. She sucked in a breath. There was pain in his expression and frustration, the same sort of anger someone who was completely lucid possessed when trapped inside of a failing body.

A blink and that was gone.

The crisp smile he shot her way was malevolent—*evil.*

Not Tyler.

"Kill him," Elisabeth said again.

The next violet strand that shot across the clearing didn't

surprise Daughtry. Not this time. Because she'd finally locked on the target doing the most damage.

Except instead of meeting with flesh, instead of creating a burst of ash, her violet magic disappeared as it collided with a barrier several inches from Elisabeth's body. She raised a brow at Daughtry, and turned back to Tyler. "Kill. Him." It was an insidious order. One that prompted Tyler into motion.

Cody put his hands up as his friend raised the blade for the third time. "I won't fight you."

"What?" she all but screamed. *"Fight him! You have to."*

"Trust me."

Daughtry clenched her fists until her nails bit sharply into her palms. Of course he'd chosen the two words that she was unable to rebut. Because he was regaining her trust brick by brick, because he had learned to have faith in her in return.

"Fight it," Cody said, his hands raised in a gesture of surrender.

"Don't," Dante said and took a step forward.

"No," Cody said. "Wait."

Tyler lunged and Daughtry's sharp exhale bordered on a scream. She clamped a hand over her mouth to prevent further sounds.

It didn't matter. Cody was faster. A simple, controlled movement and he was out of harm's way.

"Don't Tyler," he said. "Fight the darkness. Come back."

Another slash. Another dodge.

Cody tripped.

Tyler was on him in a heartbeat, his blade slicing through the air. In Daughtry's eyes, the motion seemed to be in both fast-forward and slow motion.

"No!" she yelled across the bond, her feet already moving.

Too late.

The silver blade was less than an inch from Cody's chest.

Daughtry caught movement out of the corner of her eye, saw the LexTals diving towards the pair.

It wouldn't matter.

She stumbled, her eyes locked on the knife, sure that any second she would watch it penetrate Cody's chest, pierce his heart.

Even he couldn't heal that fast.

But the blade never penetrated.

Not Cody, at least.

Tyler grunted as he ran the sharp metal across one thigh, and severed the thick artery in his upper leg.

Blood spurted, bright red, but foul-smelling.

Daughtry sprinted to Tyler's side. Cody grabbed her arm and tried to pull her back, but she wasn't having it because Tyler—*her* Tyler—was free of whatever monster had held him.

His bright blue eyes were dulled with pain, his skin ashy and clammy.

"The Dalshie—" He broke off on a gasp. "Colony . . ."

"Hey. It's okay," she said, kneeling next to him, pressing her hands to his leg. He'd wounded himself deeply, and Cody's hold on his blood was tenuous. *"You have him?"* she thought.

He nodded. *"A half a second later and he would have been dead."*

Tyler groaned. "Want . . . O–orb."

"I don't understand," she said. "The Dalshie want something or are they coming for the Colony?"

Tyler nodded.

Cody's horror hit her across the bond. He glanced to Dante but the LexTal leader's eyes were on Elisabeth.

Daughtry watched as well, and was terrified to see the calm curiosity with which Elisabeth regarded them.

"Heal yourself," Cody said, his teeth gritted, his forehead gleaming with sweat. "I've got your blood. I can't heal you too."

The bolt of black shocked everyone.

The hairs on her arms rose as it neared her. She watched the magic come, unable to find the correct action, lacking the instinct to prevent it from striking her.

Daughtry could almost feel the way it would tear her skin and burn through her nerve endings. It would be frozen fire, activating every pain center in her body.

She'd never been hit by dark magic before, but she'd felt the agony in Cody's memories. The shield surrounding her wouldn't protect her from it, hadn't been calibrated to do so. Hadn't *needed* to protect her in that way.

Cody dove in front of her.

Ebony ricocheted off of emerald.

The bolt bounced harmlessly off into the atmosphere.

Something hot hit Daughtry in the face.

Her eyes flew downwards.

She dove for the wound on Tyler's leg, desperate to put pressure on it, to stymie the flow.

It was beyond help. In his effort to save her, Cody had lost his hold on Tyler's blood.

Red flowed, stained the green grass a deathly brown.

—Phoenix Freed, the conclusion of the Phoenix Series, is now available.

PHOENIX SERIES

Phoenix Rising

Dark Phoenix

Phoenix Freed

ALSO BY ELISE FABER

(see a full listing and descriptions at www.elisefaber.com)

Roosevelt Ranch Series (all stand alone)

Disaster at Roosevelt Ranch

Heartbreak at Roosevelt Ranch

Collision at Roosevelt Ranch

Regret at Roosevelt Ranch

Desire at Roosevelt Ranch (November 3rd, 2019)

Billionaire's Club (all stand alone)

Bad Night Stand

Bad Breakup

Bad Husband

Bad Hookup

Bad Divorce

Bad Fiancé (Oct 6th 2019)

Bad Boyfriend (Jan 19th, 2020)

Gold Hockey (all stand alone)

Blocked

Backhand

Boarding

Benched

Breakaway

Breakout (December 15th, 2019)

Life Sucks Series (all stand alone)

Train Wreck

Phoenix Series (rereleasing October 21st, 2019)

Phoenix Rising

Dark Phoenix

Phoenix Freed

Phoenix: LexTal Chronicles (rereleasing soon, stand alone, Phoenix world)

From Ashes

KTS Series

Fire and Ice (Hurt Anthology, stand alone)

ABOUT THE AUTHOR

USA Today bestselling author, Elise Faber, loves chocolate, Star Wars, Harry Potter, and hockey (the order depending on the day and how well her team -- the Sharks! -- are playing). She and her husband also play as much hockey as they can squeeze into their schedules, so much so that their typical date night is spent on the ice. Elise is the mom to two exuberant boys and lives in Northern California. Connect with her in her Facebook group, the Fabinators or find more information about her books at www.elisefaber.com.

facebook.com/elisefaberauthor

amazon.com/author/elisefaber

bookbub.com/profile/elise-faber

instagram.com/elisefaber

goodreads.com/elisefaber

pinterest.com/elisefaberwrite